STONE ARCH BOOKS
a capstone imprint

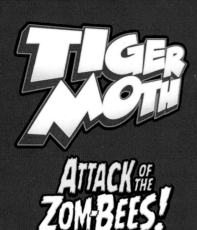

TIGER MOTH

ATTACK OF THE ZOM-BEES!

WRITTEN BY
SCOTT SONNEBORN

ILLUSTRATED BY
ANDRES ESPARZA

ASHLEY C. ANDERSEN ZANTOP .... PUBLISHER
MICHAEL DAHL .... EDITORIAL DIRECTOR
DONALD LEMKE .... EDITOR
HEATHER KINDSETH .... CREATIVE DIRECTOR
BOB LENTZ .... ART DIRECTOR
BRANN GARVEY .... SENIOR DESIGNER

STONE ARCH BOOKS
1710 ROE CREST DRIVE, NORTH MANKATO,
MINNESOTA 56003
WWW.CAPSTONEPUB.COM

CATALOGING-IN-PUBLICATION DATA IS AVAILABLE ON THE LIBRARY OF CONGRESS WEBSITE.
ISBN (HARDCOVER): 978-1-4342-3283-0
ISBN (PAPERBACK): 978-1-4342-3871-9
ISBN (E-BOOK): 978-1-4342-5968-4

SUMMARY: TIGER MOTH, INSECT NINJA, IS AT THE MERCY OF ANOTHER STUDENT...BEATRICE, THE QUEEN BEE OF ANTENNAE ELEMENTARY SCHOOL. TIGER THINKS SHE'S THE BEE'S KNEES AND OBEYS HER EVERY COMMAND–NO MATTER HOW WICKED. IN FACT, THIS KILLER BEE HAS TURNED THE ENTIRE SCHOOL INTO A BUMBLING SWARM OF ZOM-BEES! TO STOP BEATRICE AND HER DRONES, TIGER'S APPRENTICE, KUNG POW, MUST FIRST DEFEAT HIS OWN MASTER.

PRINTED IN THE UNITED STATES IN
STEVENS POINT, WISCONSIN.
092012 006937WZS13

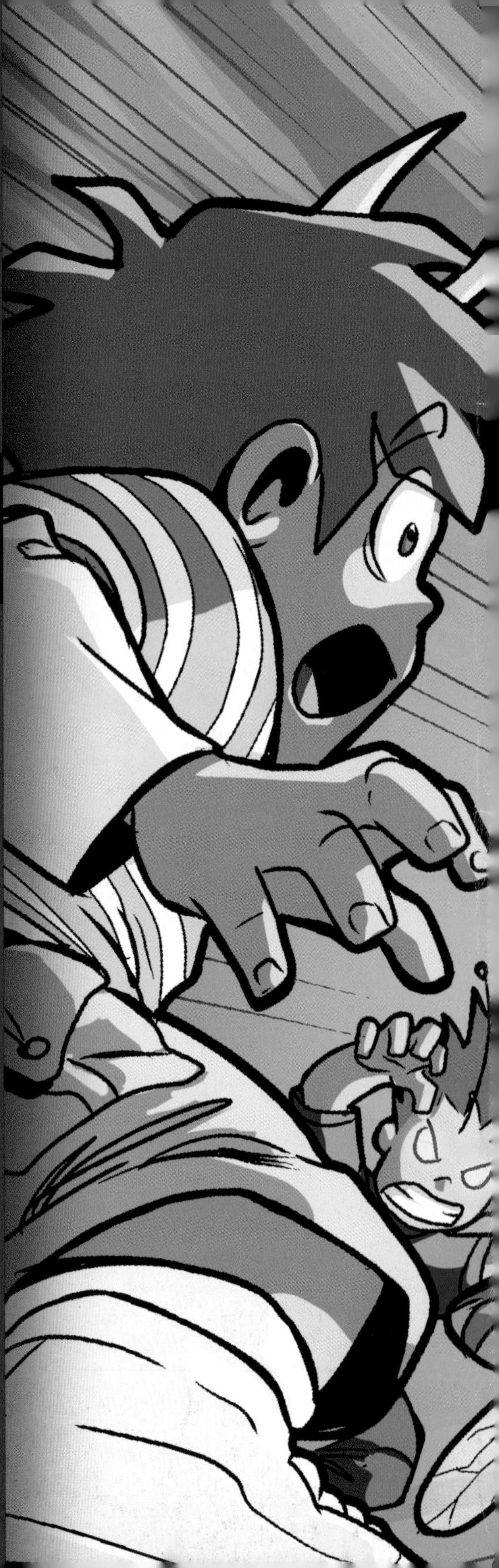

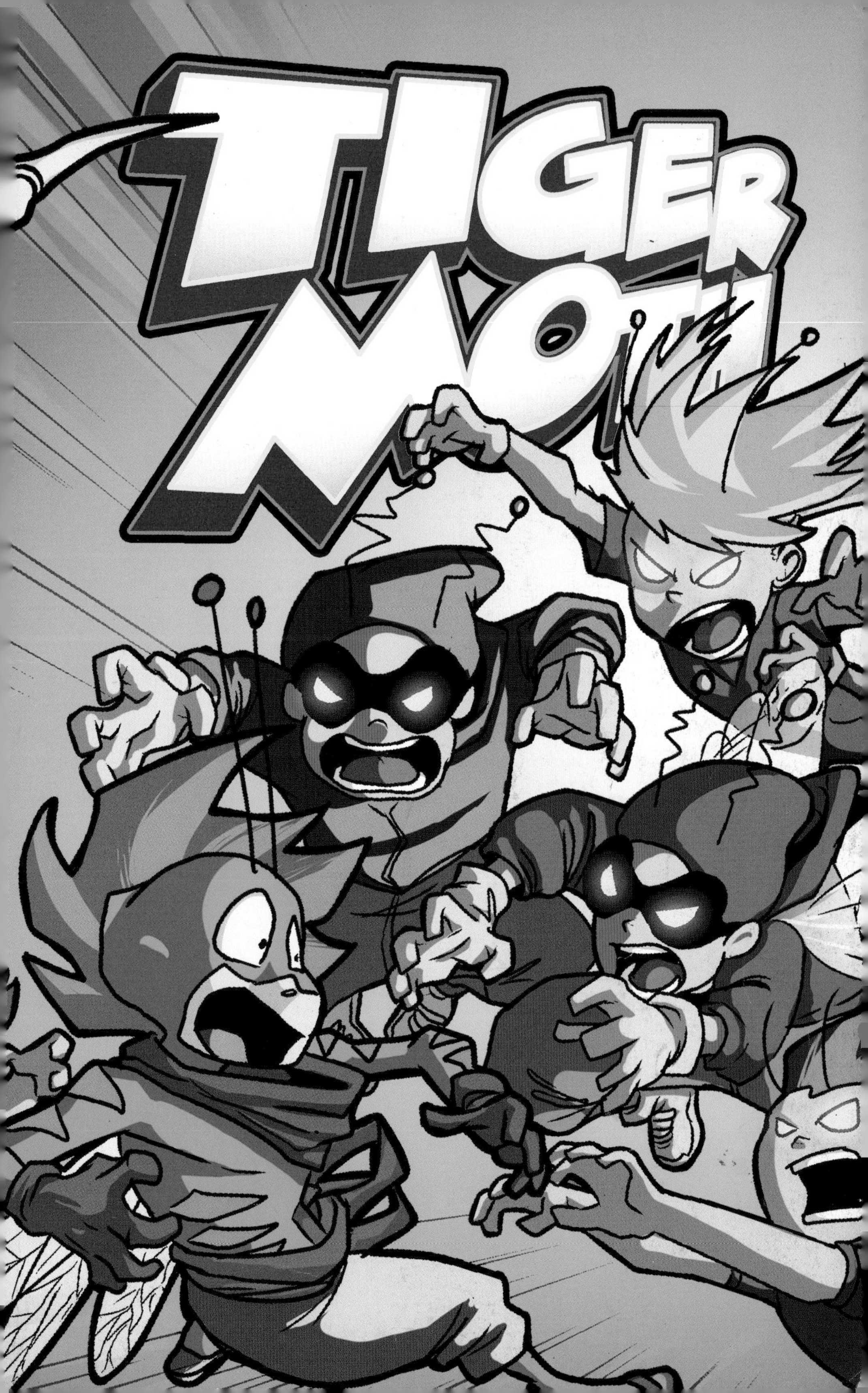
TIGER

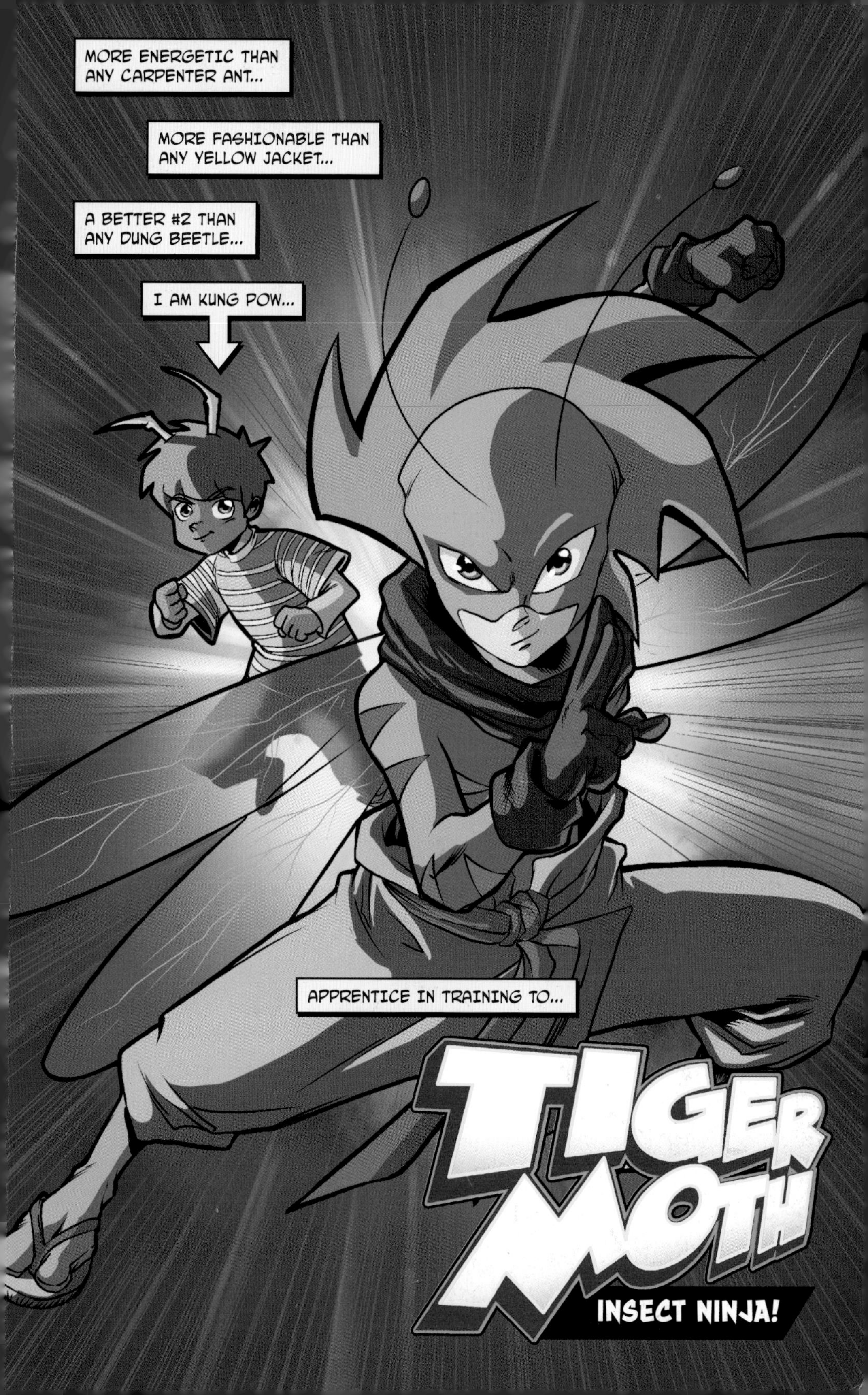
MORE ENERGETIC THAN ANY CARPENTER ANT...
MORE FASHIONABLE THAN ANY YELLOW JACKET...
A BETTER #2 THAN ANY DUNG BEETLE...
I AM KUNG POW...
APPRENTICE IN TRAINING TO...
TIGER MOTH
INSECT NINJA!

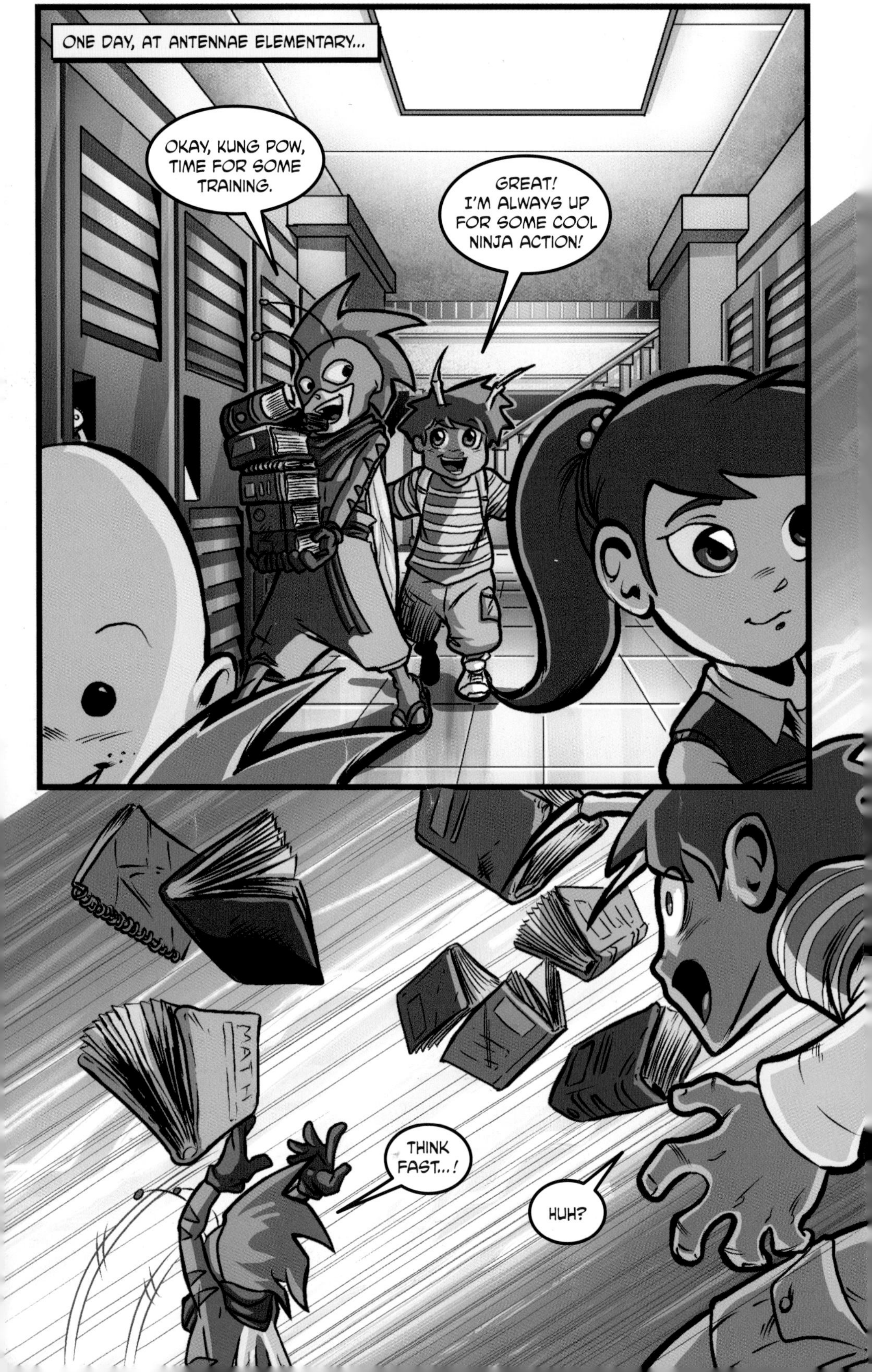
ONE DAY, AT ANTENNAE ELEMENTARY...
OKAY, KUNG POW, TIME FOR SOME TRAINING.
GREAT! I'M ALWAYS UP FOR SOME COOL NINJA ACTION!
MATH
THINK FAST...!
HUH?

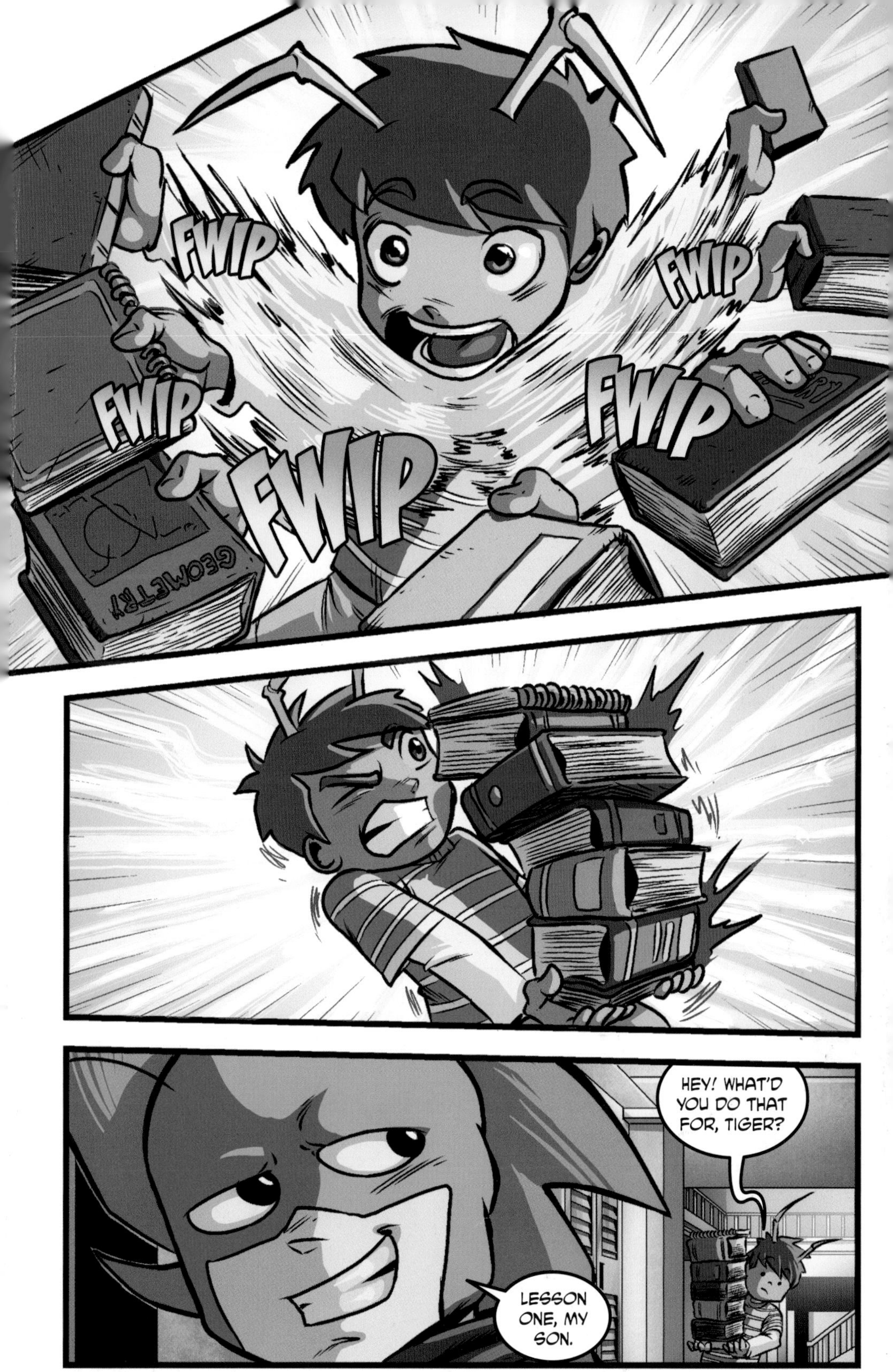
FWIP
FWIP
FWIP
FWIP
FWIP
GEOMETRY
HEY! WHAT'D YOU DO THAT FOR, TIGER?
LESSON ONE, MY SON.

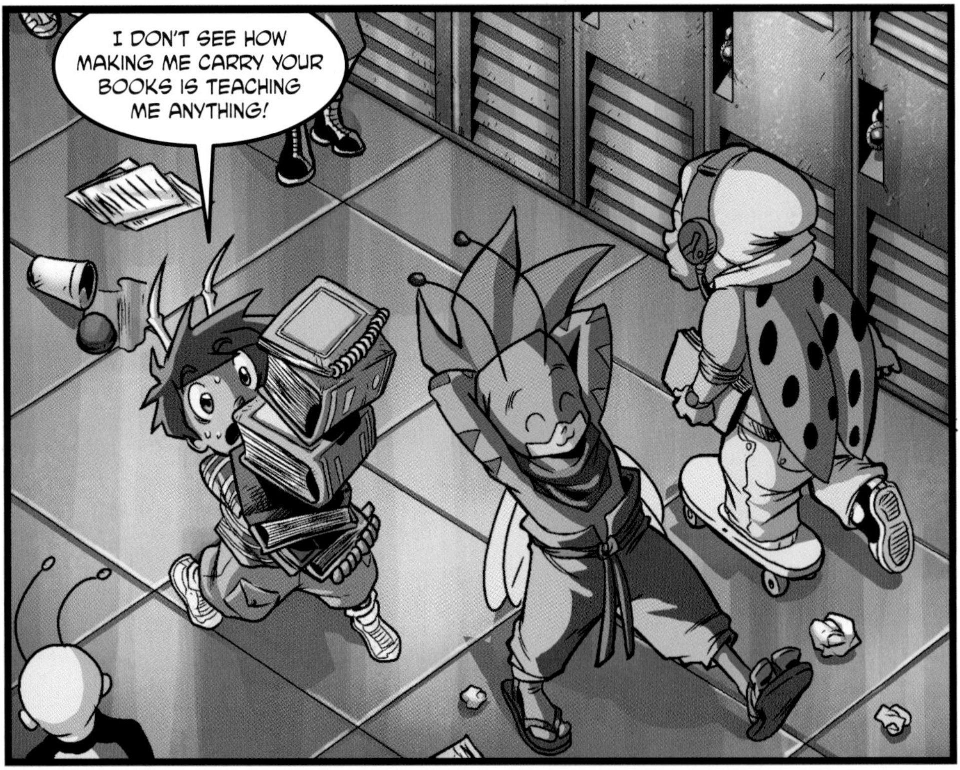
I DON'T SEE HOW MAKING ME CARRY YOUR BOOKS IS TEACHING ME ANYTHING!

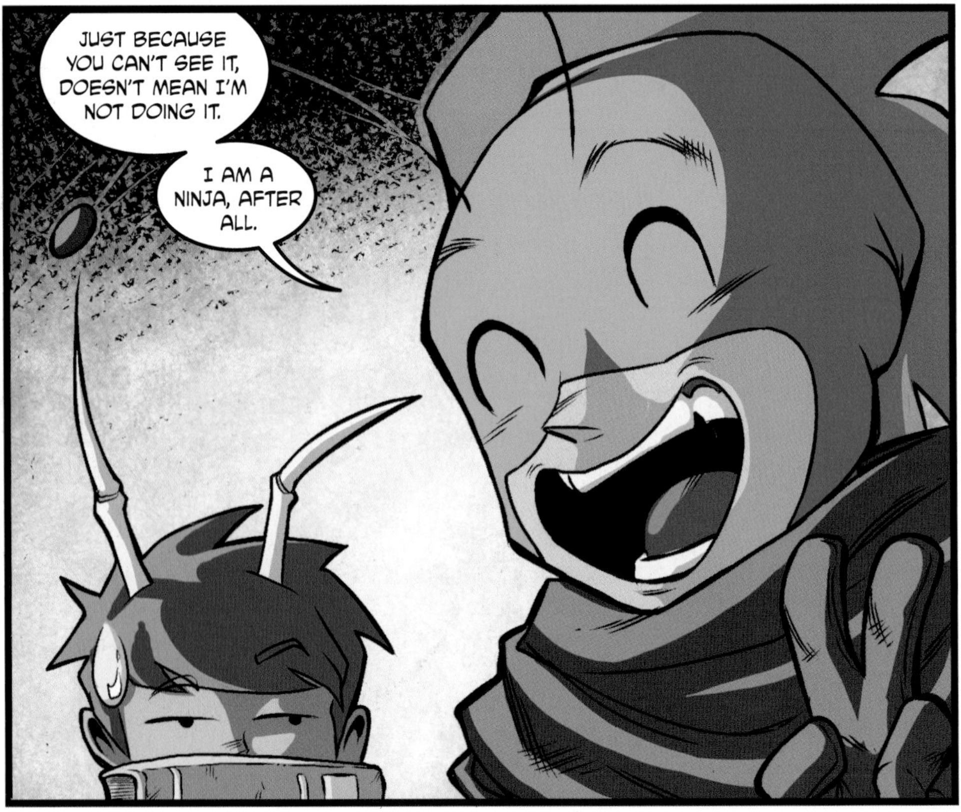
JUST BECAUSE YOU CAN'T SEE IT, DOESN'T MEAN I'M NOT DOING IT.
I AM A NINJA, AFTER ALL.

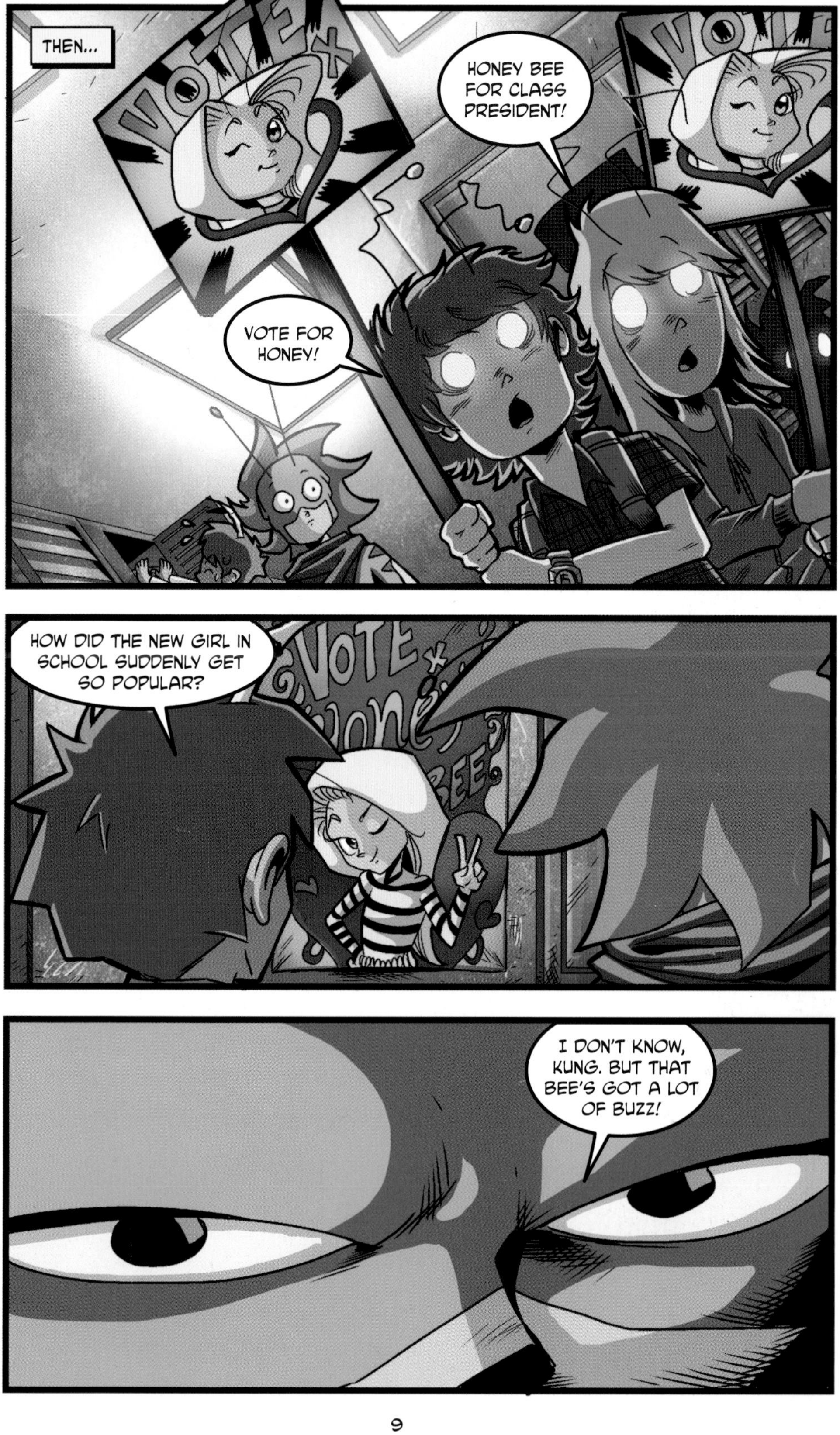
THEN...
HONEY BEE FOR CLASS PRESIDENT!
VOTE FOR HONEY!
HOW DID THE NEW GIRL IN SCHOOL SUDDENLY GET SO POPULAR?
I DON'T KNOW, KUNG. BUT THAT BEE'S GOT A LOT OF BUZZ!

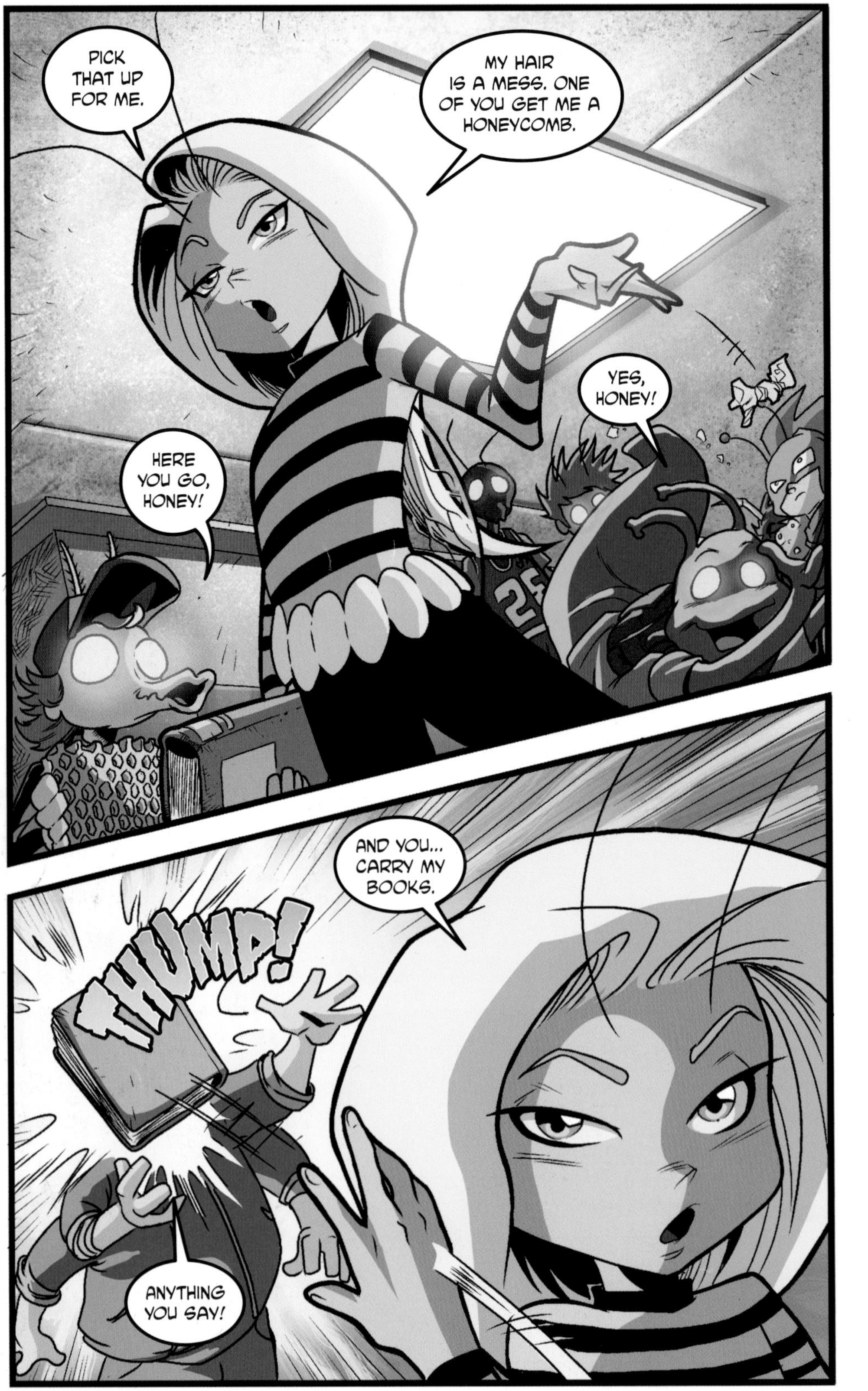
PICK THAT UP FOR ME.
MY HAIR IS A MESS. ONE OF YOU GET ME A HONEYCOMB.
YES, HONEY!
HERE YOU GO, HONEY!
AND YOU... CARRY MY BOOKS.
THUMP!
ANYTHING YOU SAY!

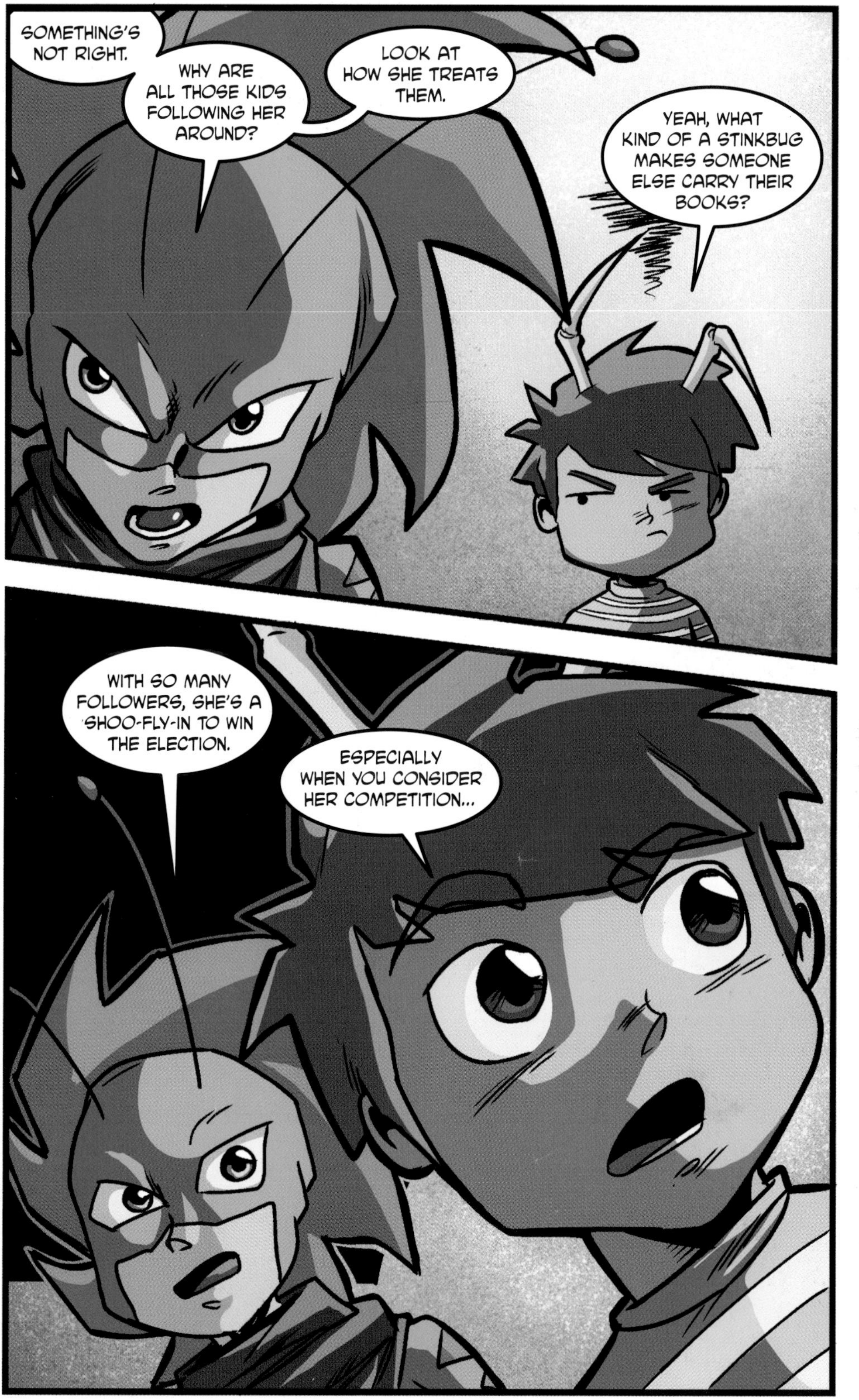
SOMETHING'S NOT RIGHT.
WHY ARE ALL THOSE KIDS FOLLOWING HER AROUND?
LOOK AT HOW SHE TREATS THEM.
YEAH, WHAT KIND OF A STINKBUG MAKES SOMEONE ELSE CARRY THEIR BOOKS?
WITH SO MANY FOLLOWERS, SHE'S A SHOO-FLY-IN TO WIN THE ELECTION.
ESPECIALLY WHEN YOU CONSIDER HER COMPETITION...

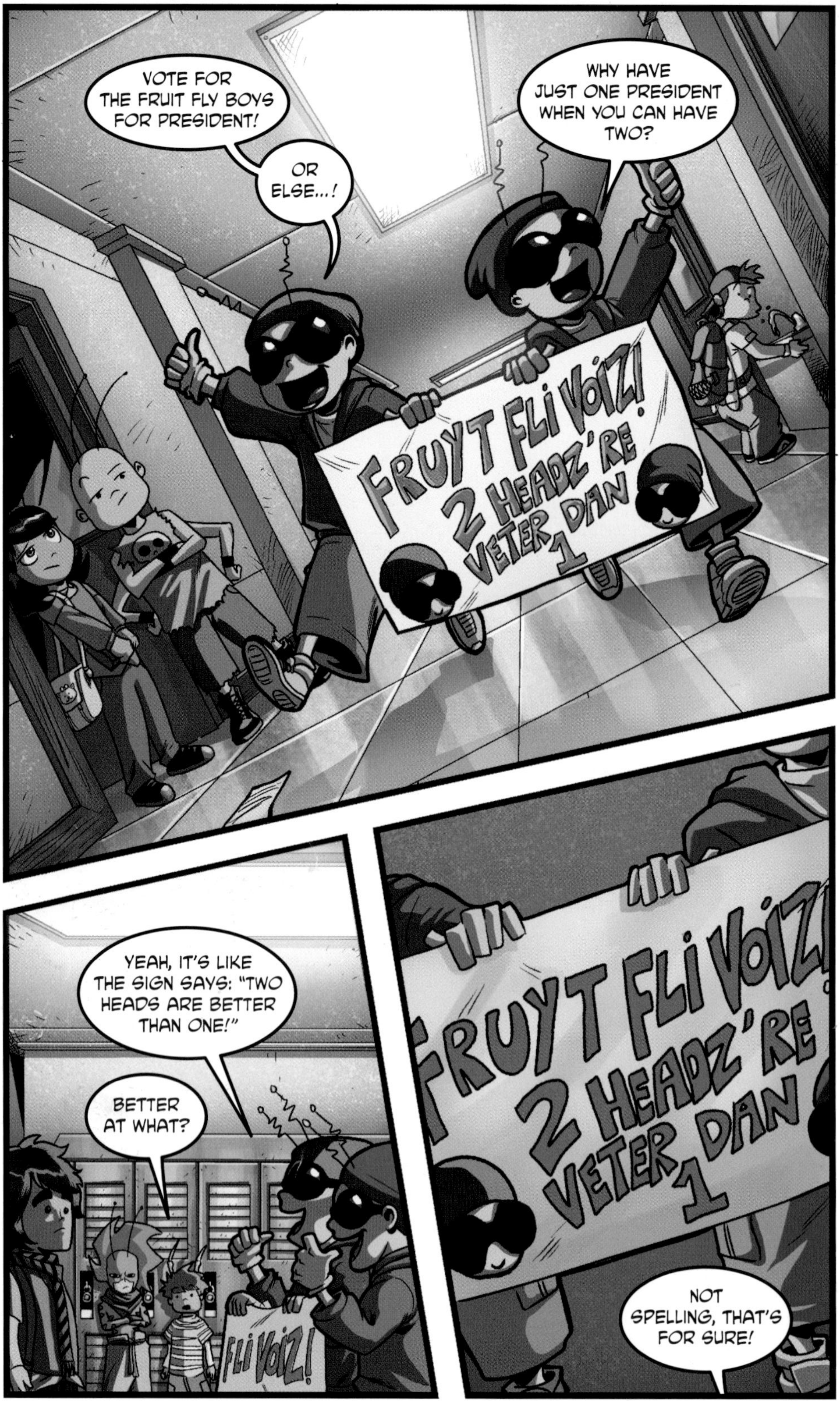
VOTE FOR THE FRUIT FLY BOYS FOR PRESIDENT!
OR ELSE...!
WHY HAVE JUST ONE PRESIDENT WHEN YOU CAN HAVE TWO?
FRUYT FLI VOIZ!
2 HEADZ'RE VETER DAN 1
YEAH, IT'S LIKE THE SIGN SAYS: "TWO HEADS ARE BETTER THAN ONE!"
BETTER AT WHAT?
FLI VOIZ!
FRUYT FLI VOIZ!
2 HEADZ'RE VETER DAN 1
NOT SPELLING, THAT'S FOR SURE!

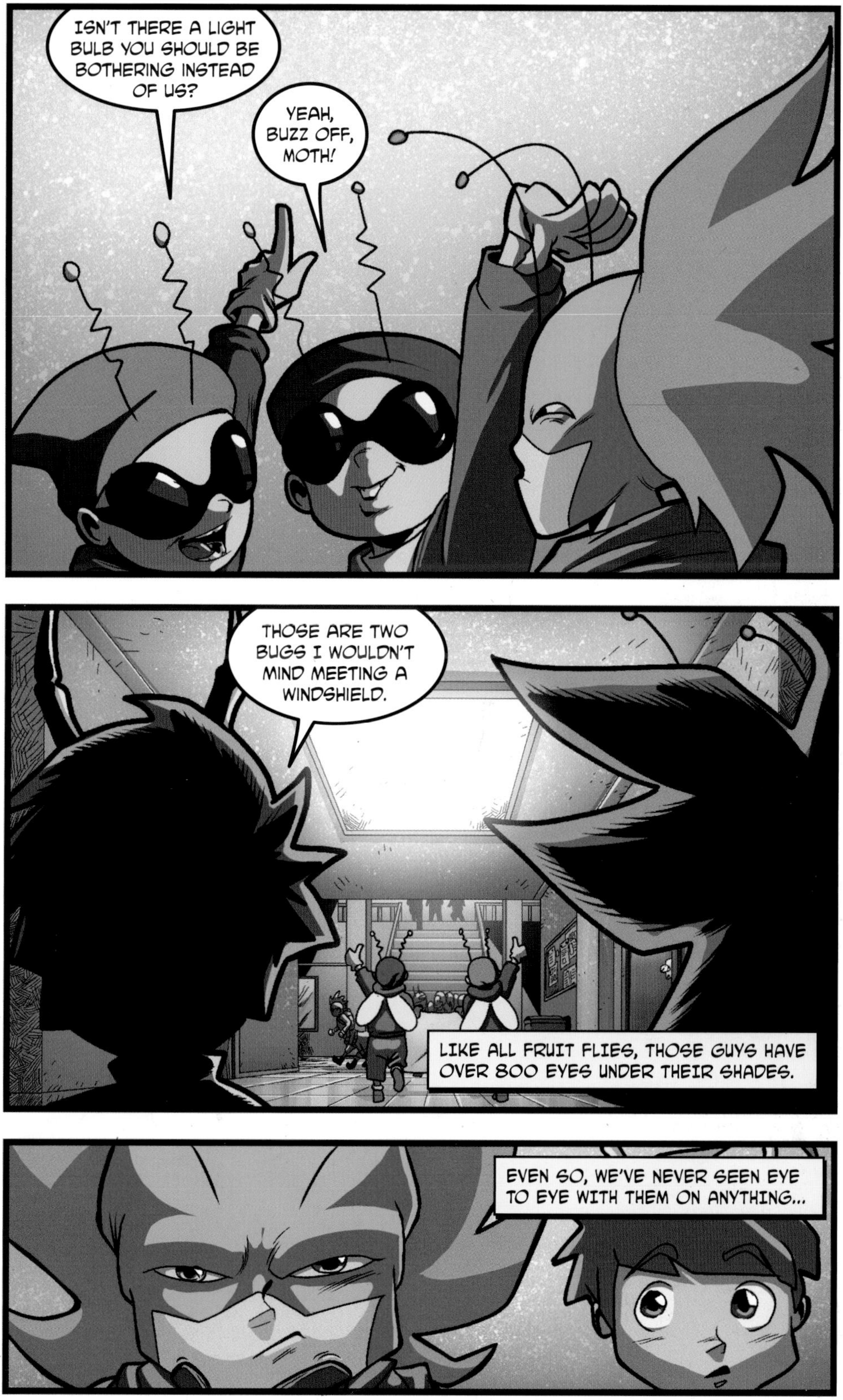
ISN'T THERE A LIGHT BULB YOU SHOULD BE BOTHERING INSTEAD OF US?
YEAH, BUZZ OFF, MOTH!
THOSE ARE TWO BUGS I WOULDN'T MIND MEETING A WINDSHIELD.
LIKE ALL FRUIT FLIES, THOSE GUYS HAVE OVER 800 EYES UNDER THEIR SHADES.
EVEN SO, WE'VE NEVER SEEN EYE TO EYE WITH THEM ON ANYTHING...

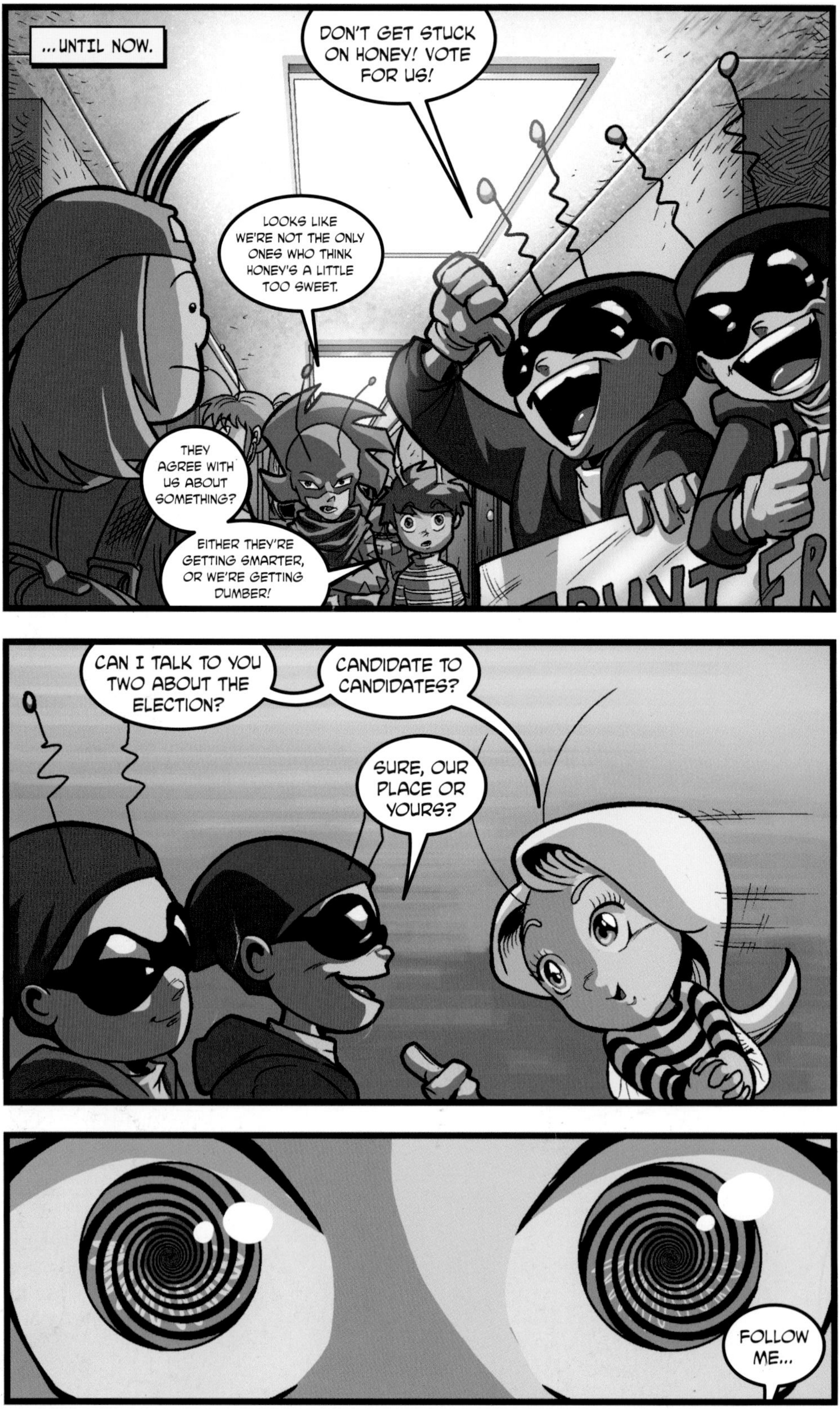
...UNTIL NOW.
DON'T GET STUCK ON HONEY! VOTE FOR US!
LOOKS LIKE WE'RE NOT THE ONLY ONES WHO THINK HONEY'S A LITTLE TOO SWEET.
THEY AGREE WITH US ABOUT SOMETHING?
EITHER THEY'RE GETTING SMARTER, OR WE'RE GETTING DUMBER!
CAN I TALK TO YOU TWO ABOUT THE ELECTION?
CANDIDATE TO CANDIDATES?
SURE, OUR PLACE OR YOURS?
FOLLOW ME...

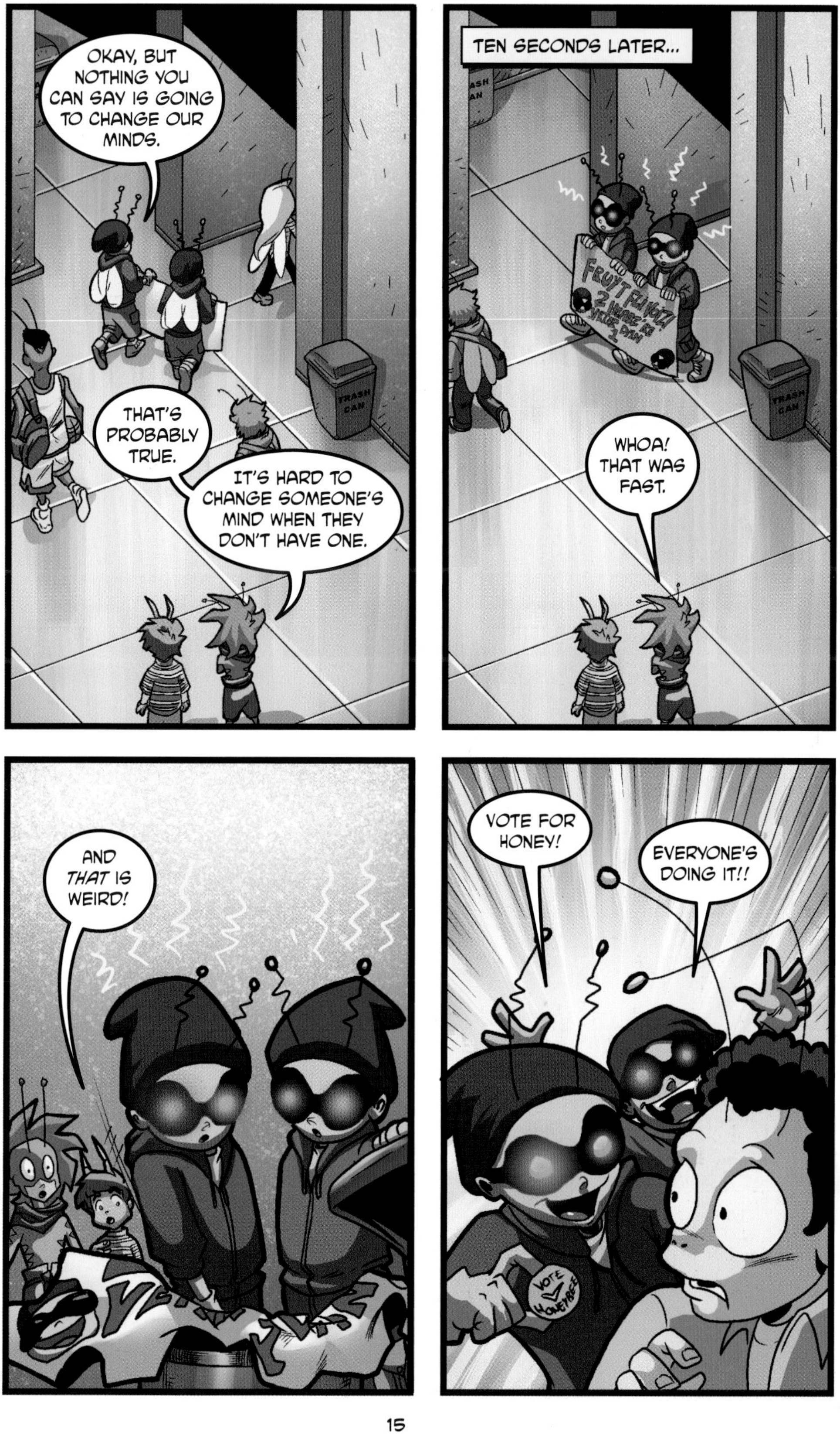
OKAY, BUT NOTHING YOU CAN SAY IS GOING TO CHANGE OUR MINDS.
TRASH CAN
THAT'S PROBABLY TRUE.
IT'S HARD TO CHANGE SOMEONE'S MIND WHEN THEY DON'T HAVE ONE.
TEN SECONDS LATER...
TRASH CAN
WHOA! THAT WAS FAST.
AND *THAT* IS WEIRD!
VOTE FOR HONEY!
EVERYONE'S DOING IT!!
VOTE HONEYBEE

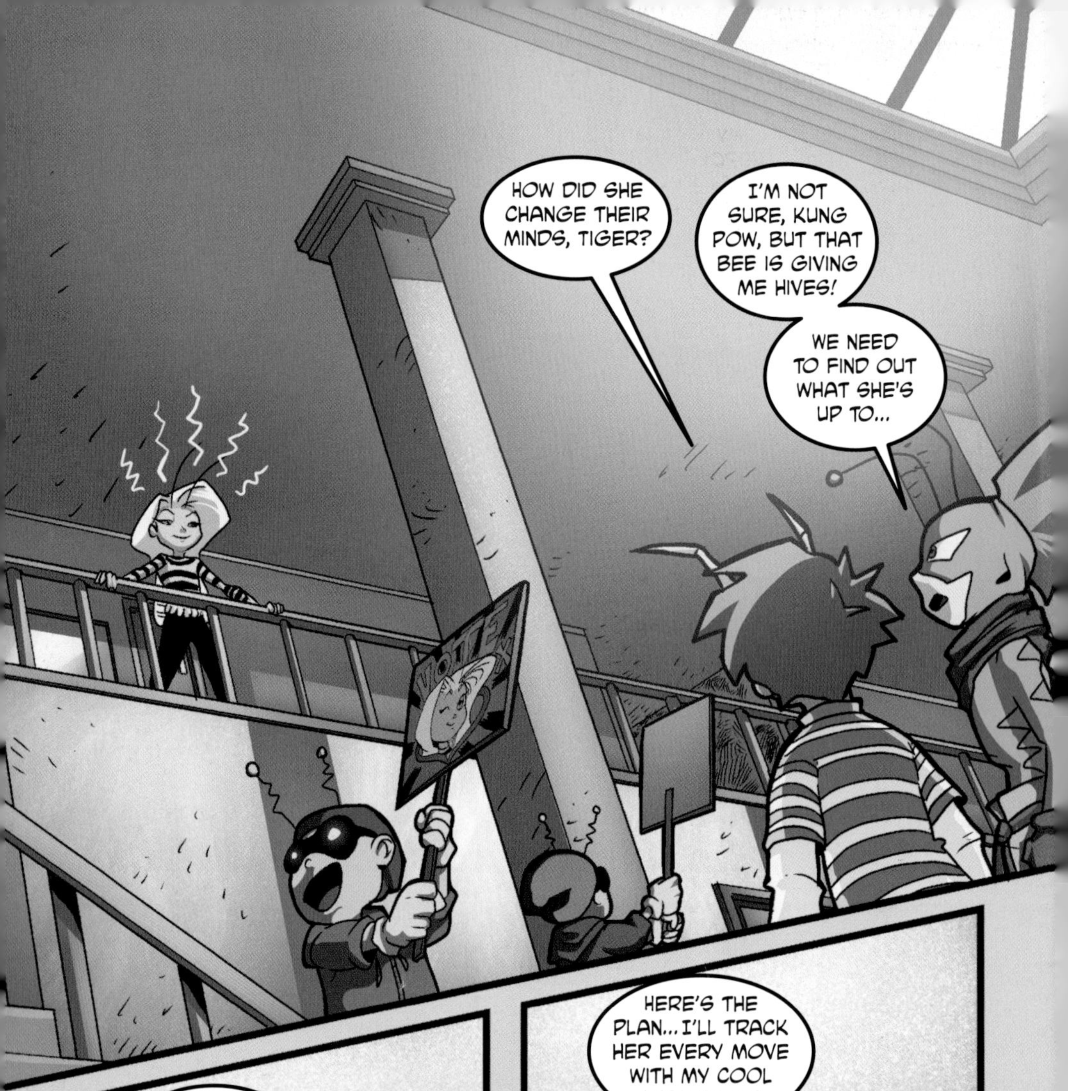
HOW DID SHE CHANGE THEIR MINDS, TIGER?
I'M NOT SURE, KUNG POW, BUT THAT BEE IS GIVING ME HIVES!
WE NEED TO FIND OUT WHAT SHE'S UP TO...

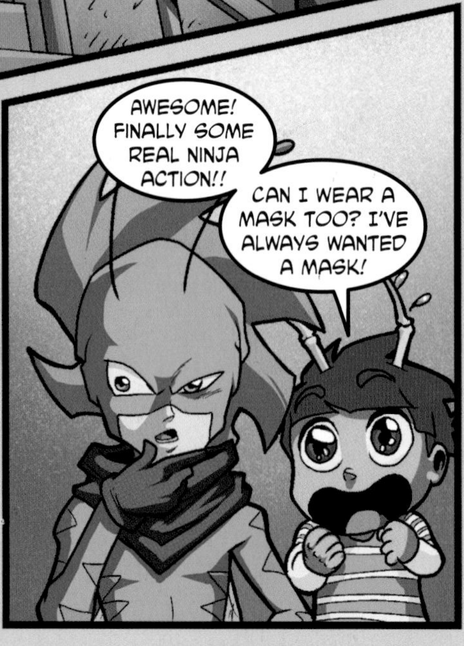
AWESOME! FINALLY SOME REAL NINJA ACTION!!
CAN I WEAR A MASK TOO? I'VE ALWAYS WANTED A MASK!

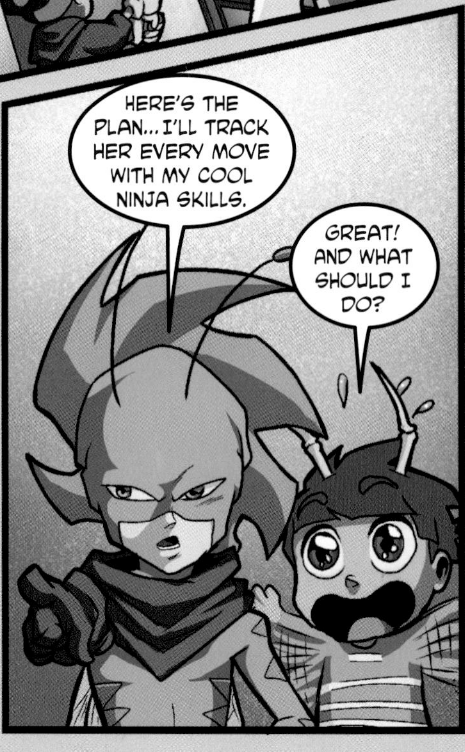
HERE'S THE PLAN... I'LL TRACK HER EVERY MOVE WITH MY COOL NINJA SKILLS.
GREAT! AND WHAT SHOULD I DO?

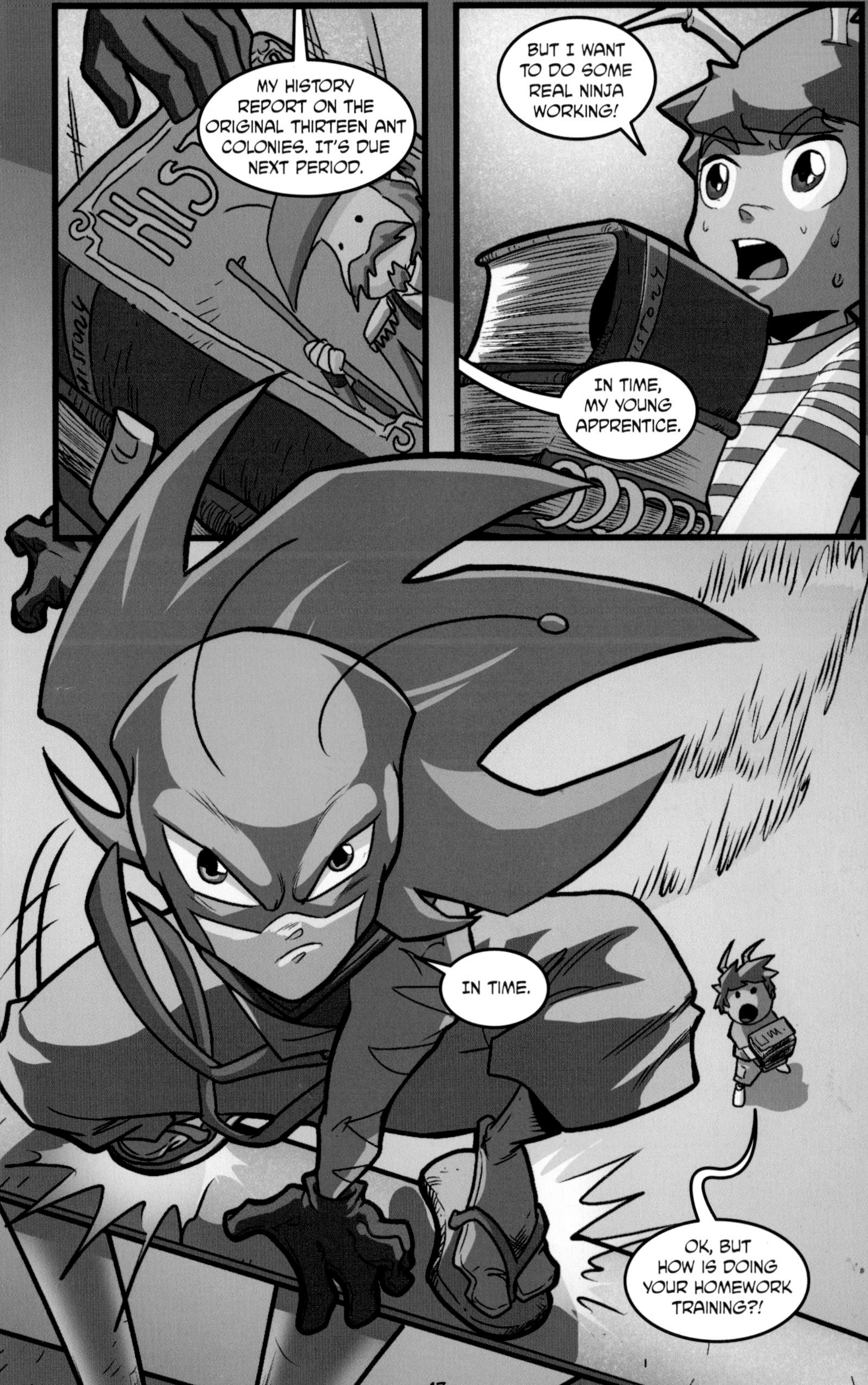
MY HISTORY REPORT ON THE ORIGINAL THIRTEEN ANT COLONIES. IT'S DUE NEXT PERIOD.
BUT I WANT TO DO SOME REAL NINJA WORKING!
IN TIME, MY YOUNG APPRENTICE.
IN TIME.
OK, BUT HOW IS DOING YOUR HOMEWORK TRAINING?!

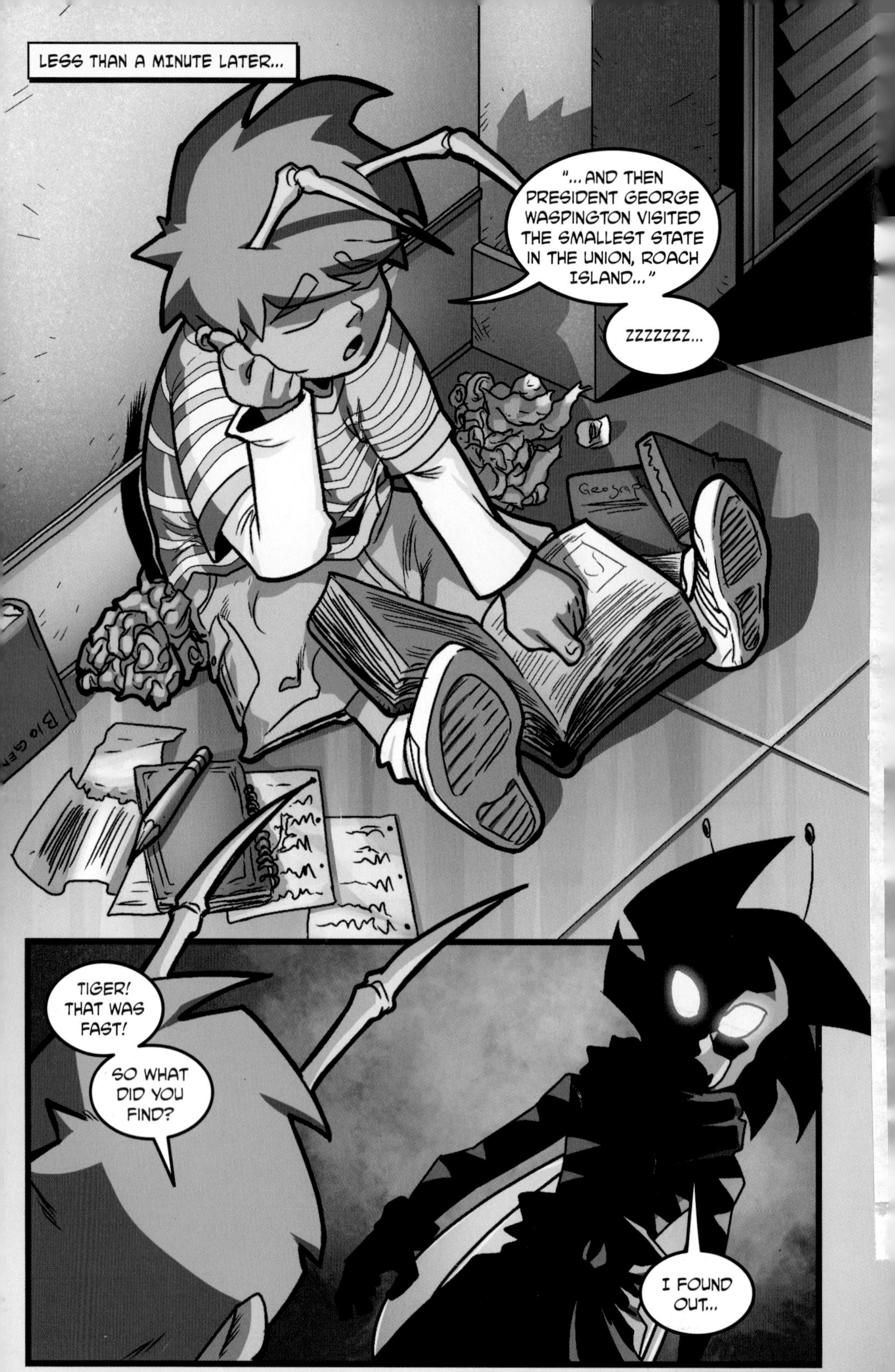
LESS THAN A MINUTE LATER...
"...AND THEN PRESIDENT GEORGE WASPINGTON VISITED THE SMALLEST STATE IN THE UNION, ROACH ISLAND..."
ZZZZZZZ...
Geograp
TIGER! THAT WAS FAST!
SO WHAT DID YOU FIND?
I FOUND OUT...

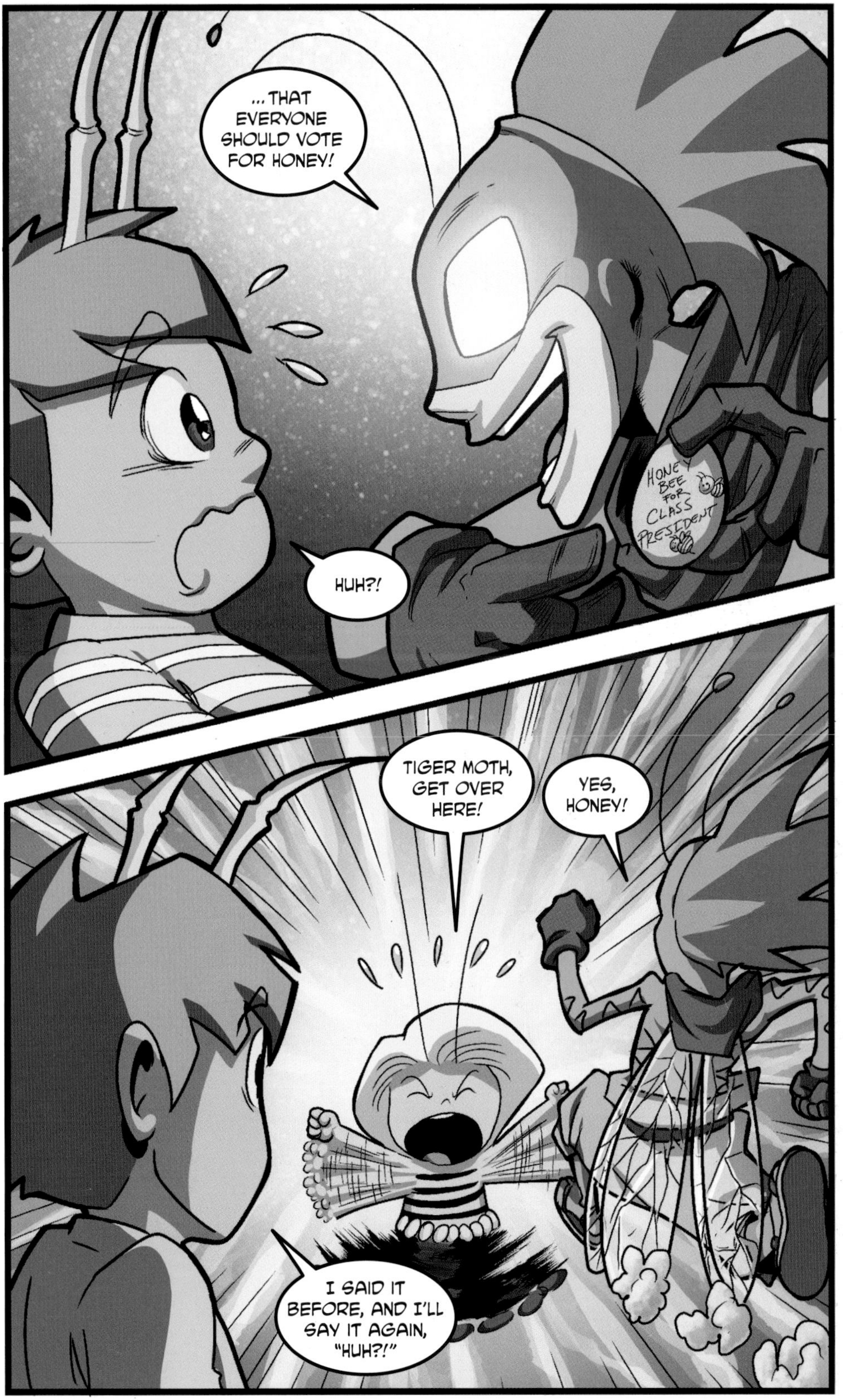
...THAT EVERYONE SHOULD VOTE FOR HONEY!
HONEY BEE FOR CLASS PRESIDENT
HUH?!
TIGER MOTH, GET OVER HERE!
YES, HONEY!
I SAID IT BEFORE, AND I'LL SAY IT AGAIN, "HUH?!"

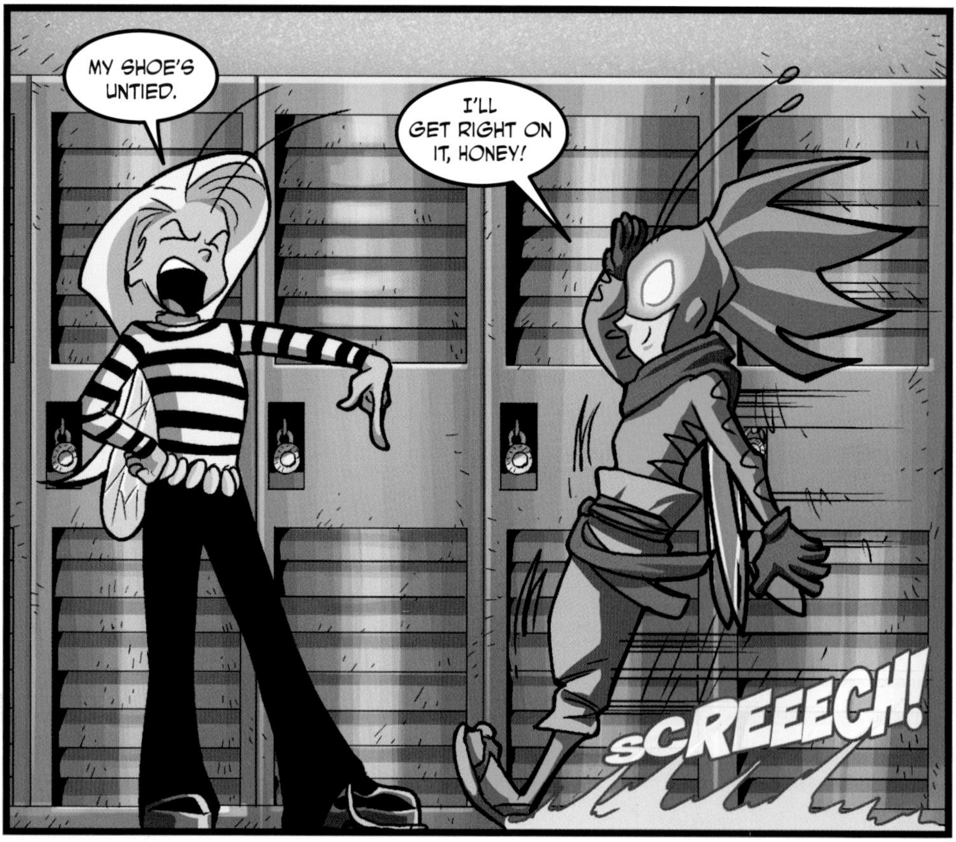
MY SHOE'S UNTIED.
I'LL GET RIGHT ON IT, HONEY!
sCREEECH!

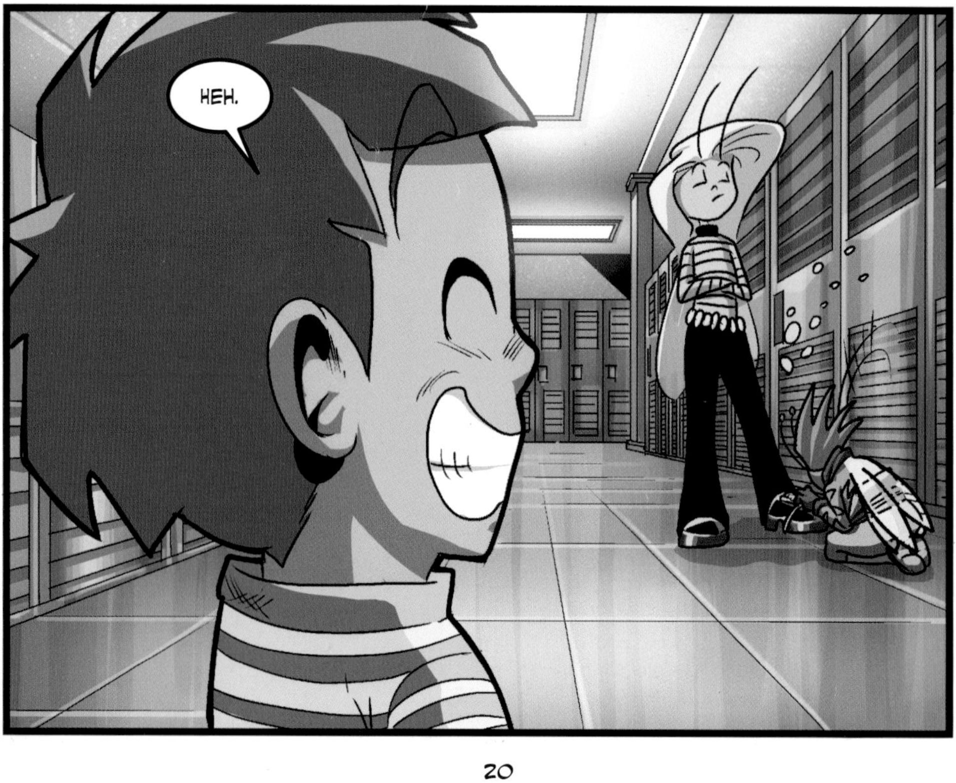
HEH.

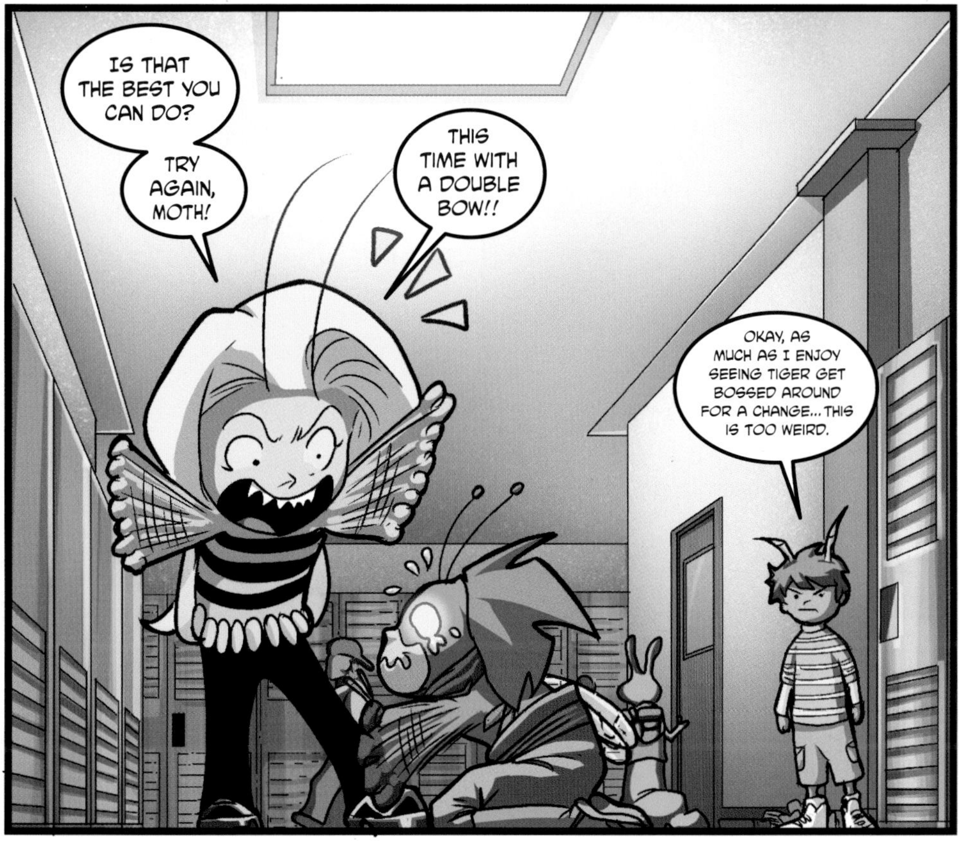
IS THAT THE BEST YOU CAN DO?
TRY AGAIN, MOTH!
THIS TIME WITH A DOUBLE BOW!!
OKAY, AS MUCH AS I ENJOY SEEING TIGER GET BOSSED AROUND FOR A CHANGE... THIS IS TOO WEIRD.

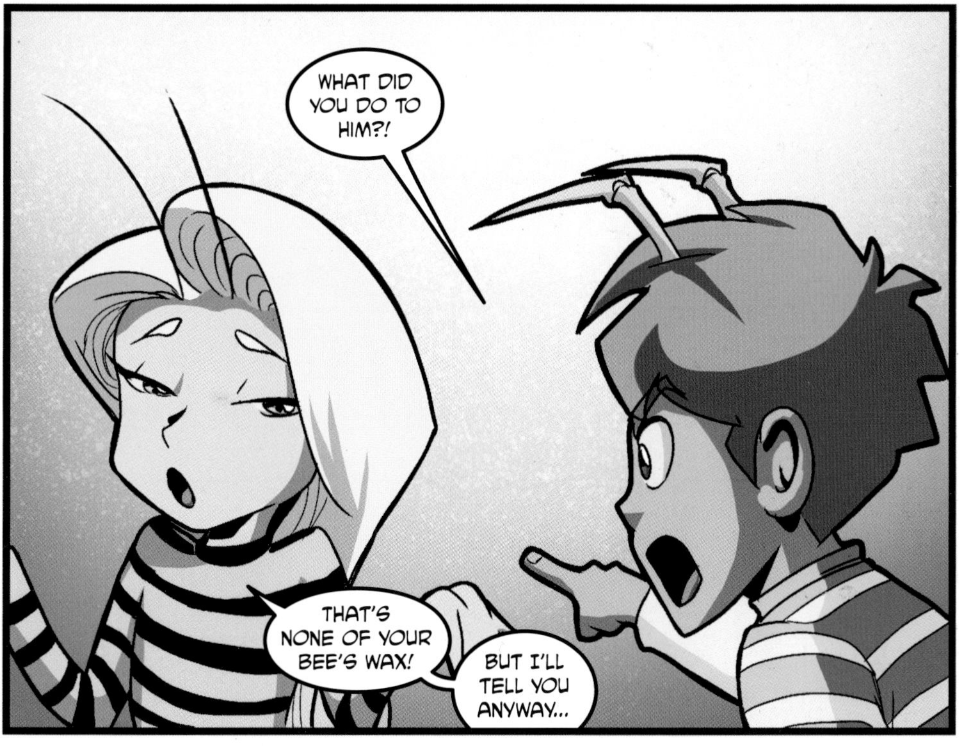
WHAT DID YOU DO TO HIM?!
THAT'S NONE OF YOUR BEE'S WAX!
BUT I'LL TELL YOU ANYWAY...

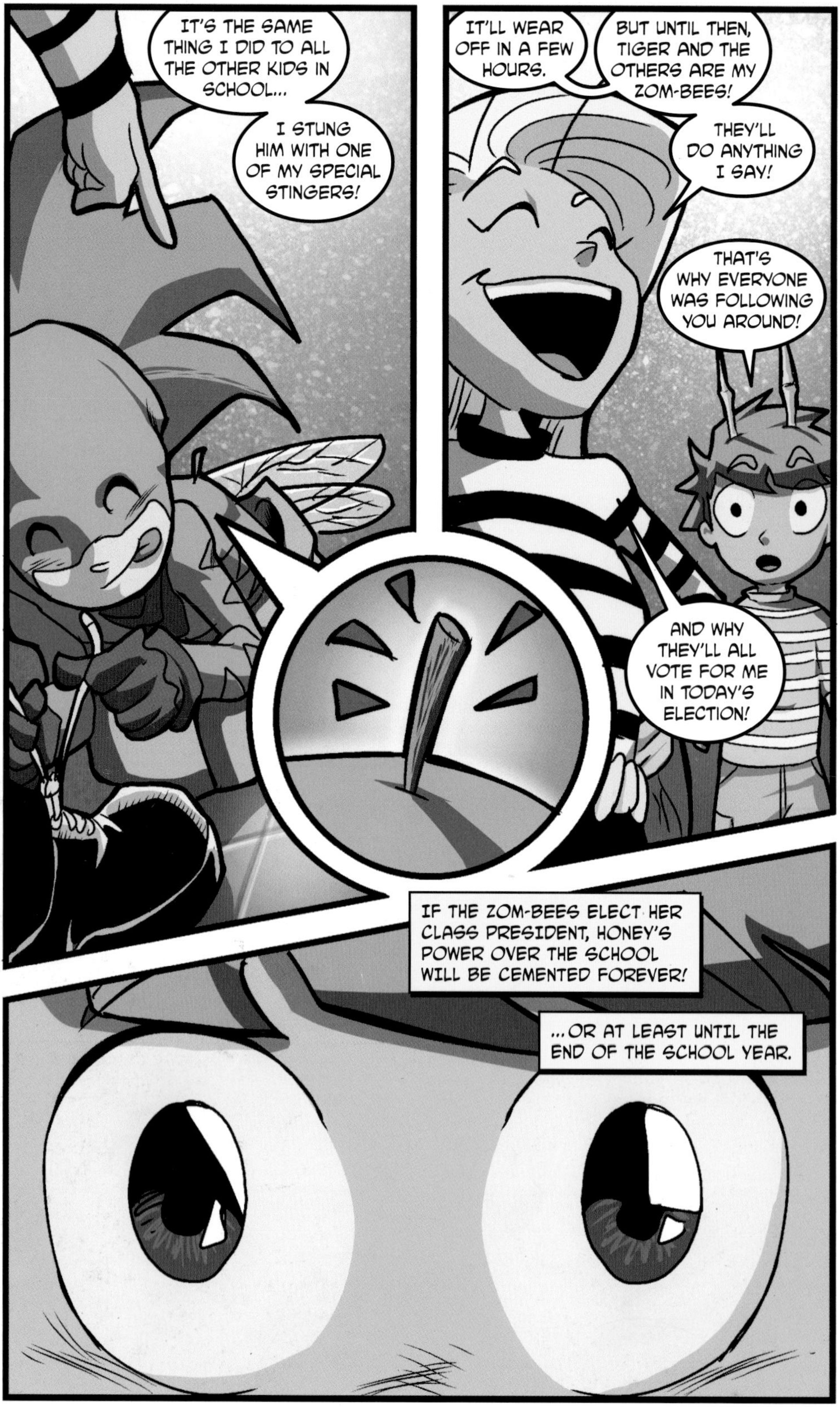
IT'S THE SAME THING I DID TO ALL THE OTHER KIDS IN SCHOOL...
I STUNG HIM WITH ONE OF MY SPECIAL STINGERS!
IT'LL WEAR OFF IN A FEW HOURS.
BUT UNTIL THEN, TIGER AND THE OTHERS ARE MY ZOM-BEES!
THEY'LL DO ANYTHING I SAY!
THAT'S WHY EVERYONE WAS FOLLOWING YOU AROUND!
AND WHY THEY'LL ALL VOTE FOR ME IN TODAY'S ELECTION!
IF THE ZOM-BEES ELECT HER CLASS PRESIDENT, HONEY'S POWER OVER THE SCHOOL WILL BE CEMENTED FOREVER!
...OR AT LEAST UNTIL THE END OF THE SCHOOL YEAR.

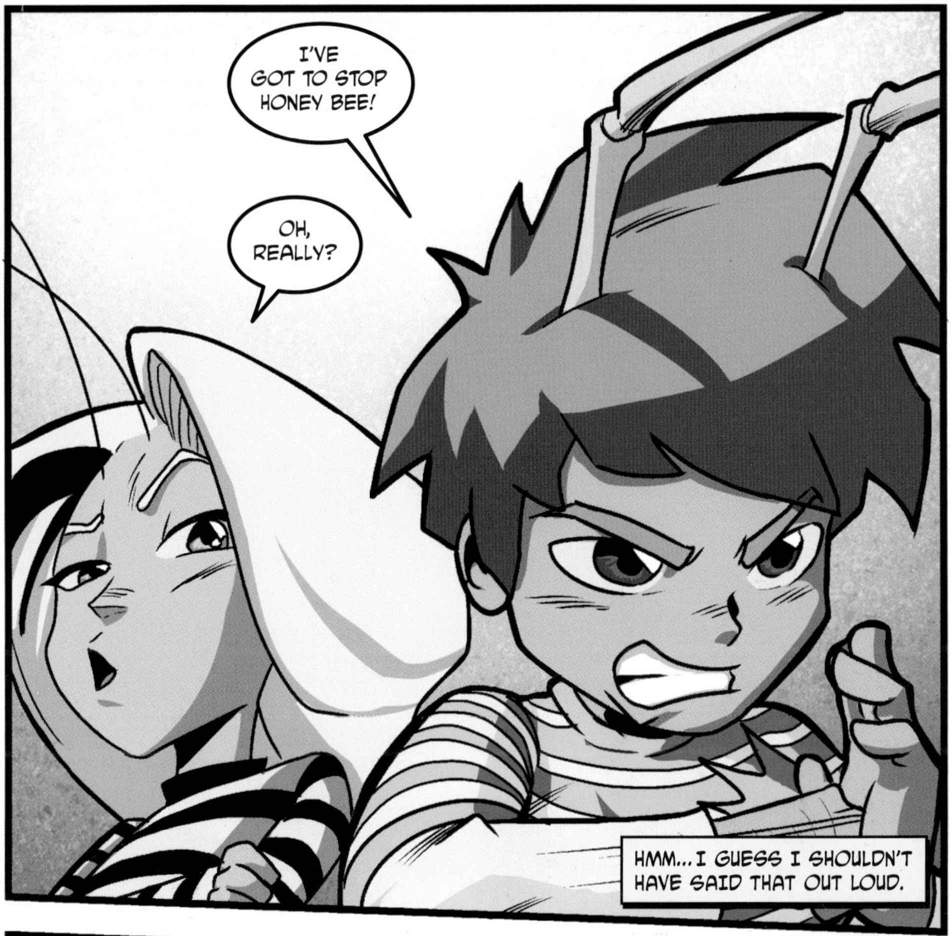
I'VE GOT TO STOP HONEY BEE!
OH, REALLY?
HMM... I GUESS I SHOULDN'T HAVE SAID THAT OUT LOUD.

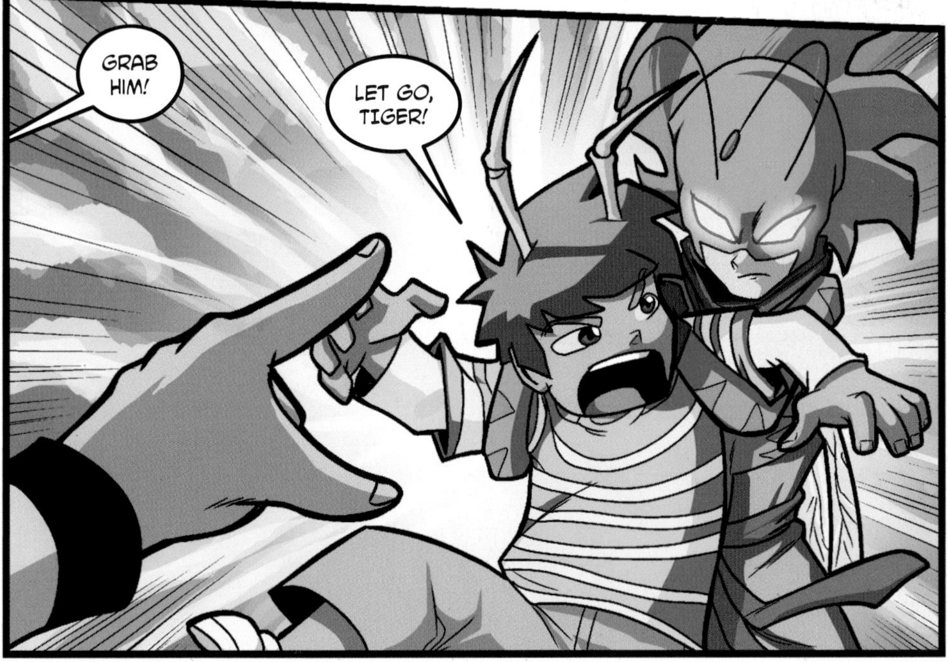
GRAB HIM!
LET GO, TIGER!

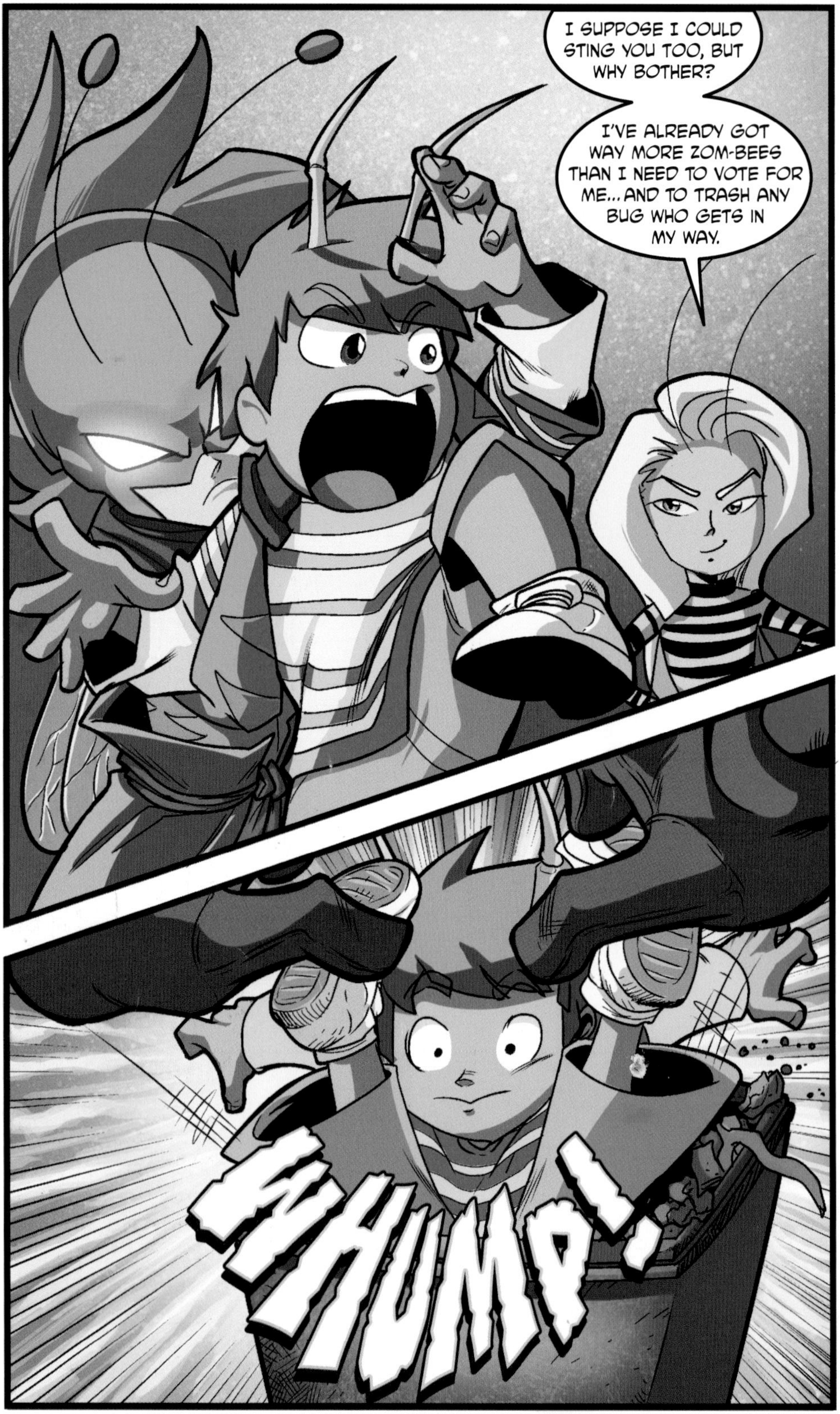
I SUPPOSE I COULD STING YOU TOO, BUT WHY BOTHER?
I'VE ALREADY GOT WAY MORE ZOM-BEES THAN I NEED TO VOTE FOR ME... AND TO TRASH ANY BUG WHO GETS IN MY WAY.
HUMP!

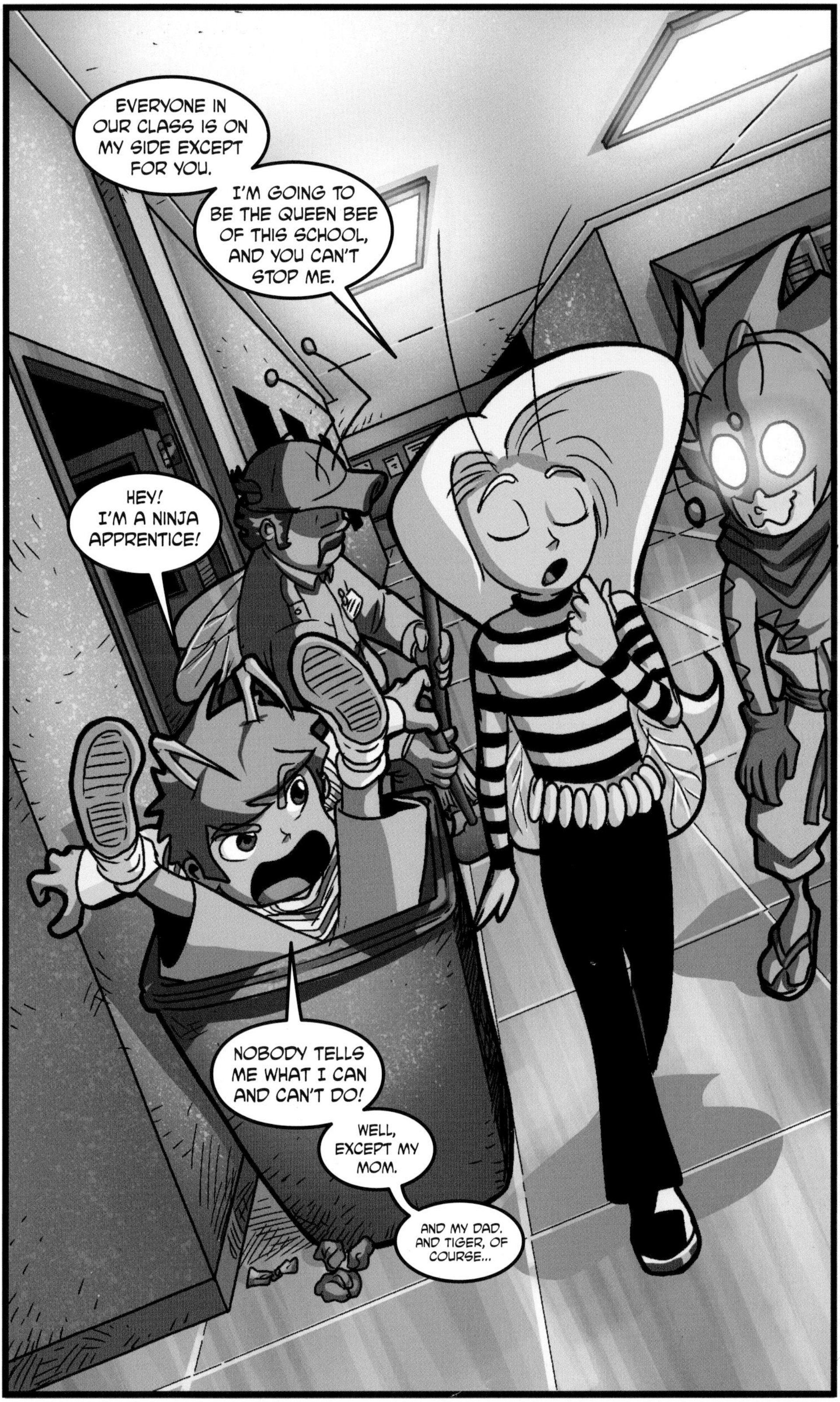
EVERYONE IN OUR CLASS IS ON MY SIDE EXCEPT FOR YOU.
I'M GOING TO BE THE QUEEN BEE OF THIS SCHOOL, AND YOU CAN'T STOP ME.
HEY! I'M A NINJA APPRENTICE!
NOBODY TELLS ME WHAT I CAN AND CAN'T DO!
WELL, EXCEPT MY MOM.
AND MY DAD. AND TIGER, OF COURSE...

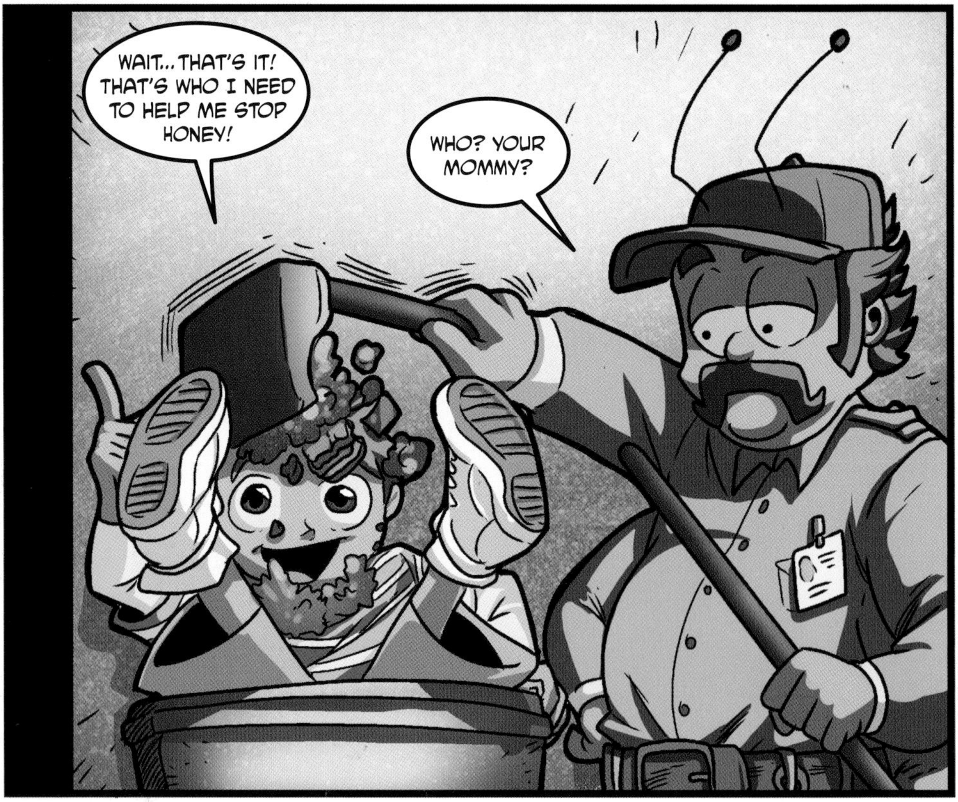
WAIT... THAT'S IT! THAT'S WHO I NEED TO HELP ME STOP HONEY!
WHO? YOUR MOMMY?

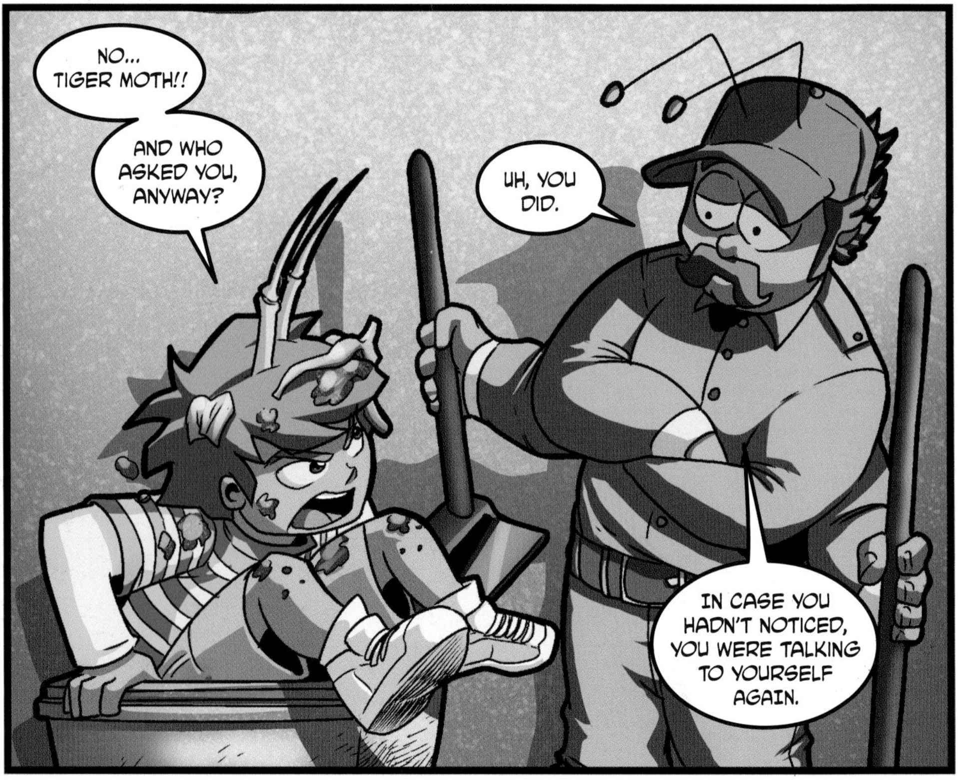
NO... TIGER MOTH!!
AND WHO ASKED YOU, ANYWAY?
UH, YOU DID.
IN CASE YOU HADN'T NOTICED, YOU WERE TALKING TO YOURSELF AGAIN.

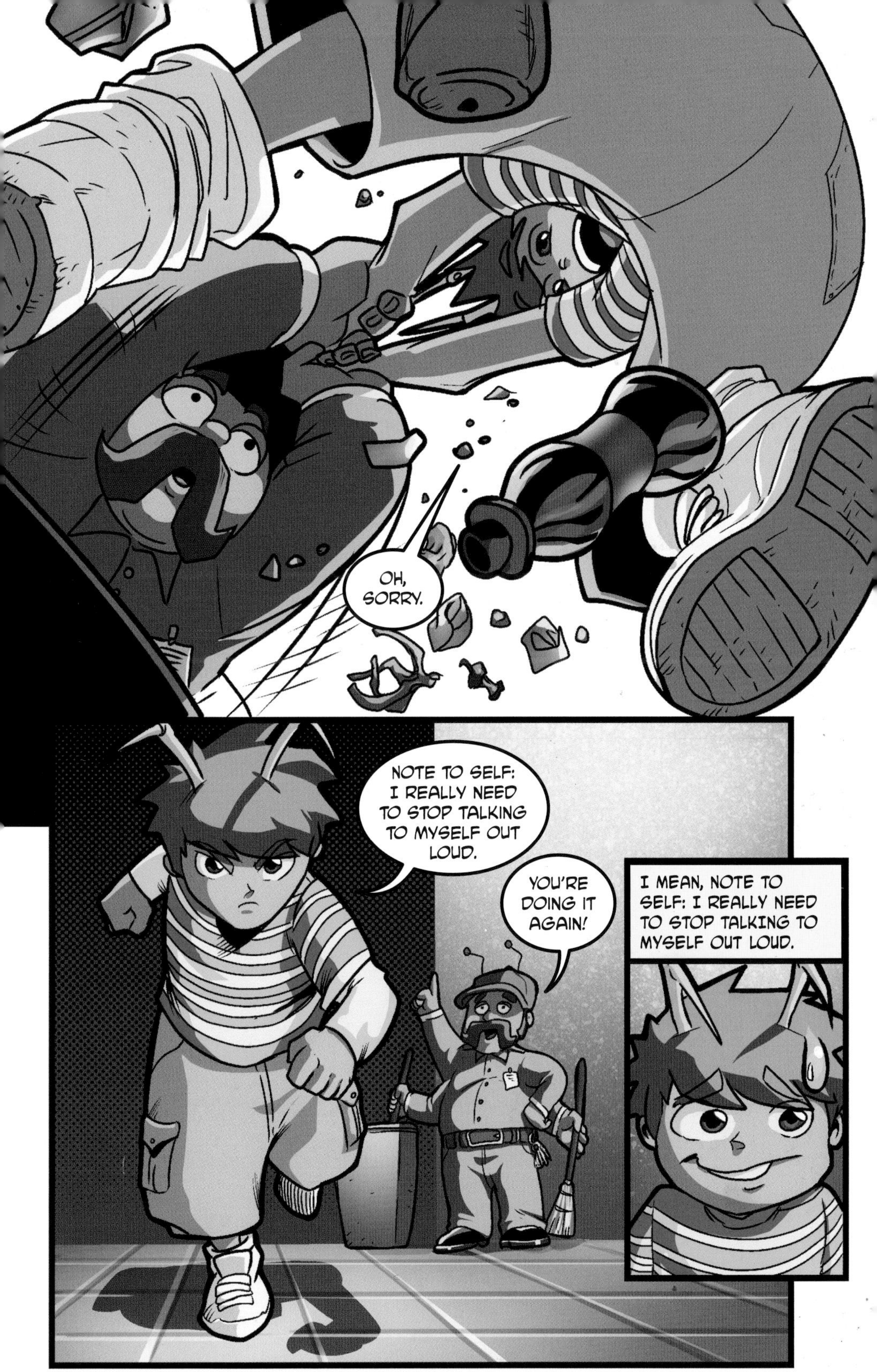
OH, SORRY.
NOTE TO SELF: I REALLY NEED TO STOP TALKING TO MYSELF OUT LOUD.
YOU'RE DOING IT AGAIN!
I MEAN, NOTE TO SELF: I REALLY NEED TO STOP TALKING TO MYSELF OUT LOUD.

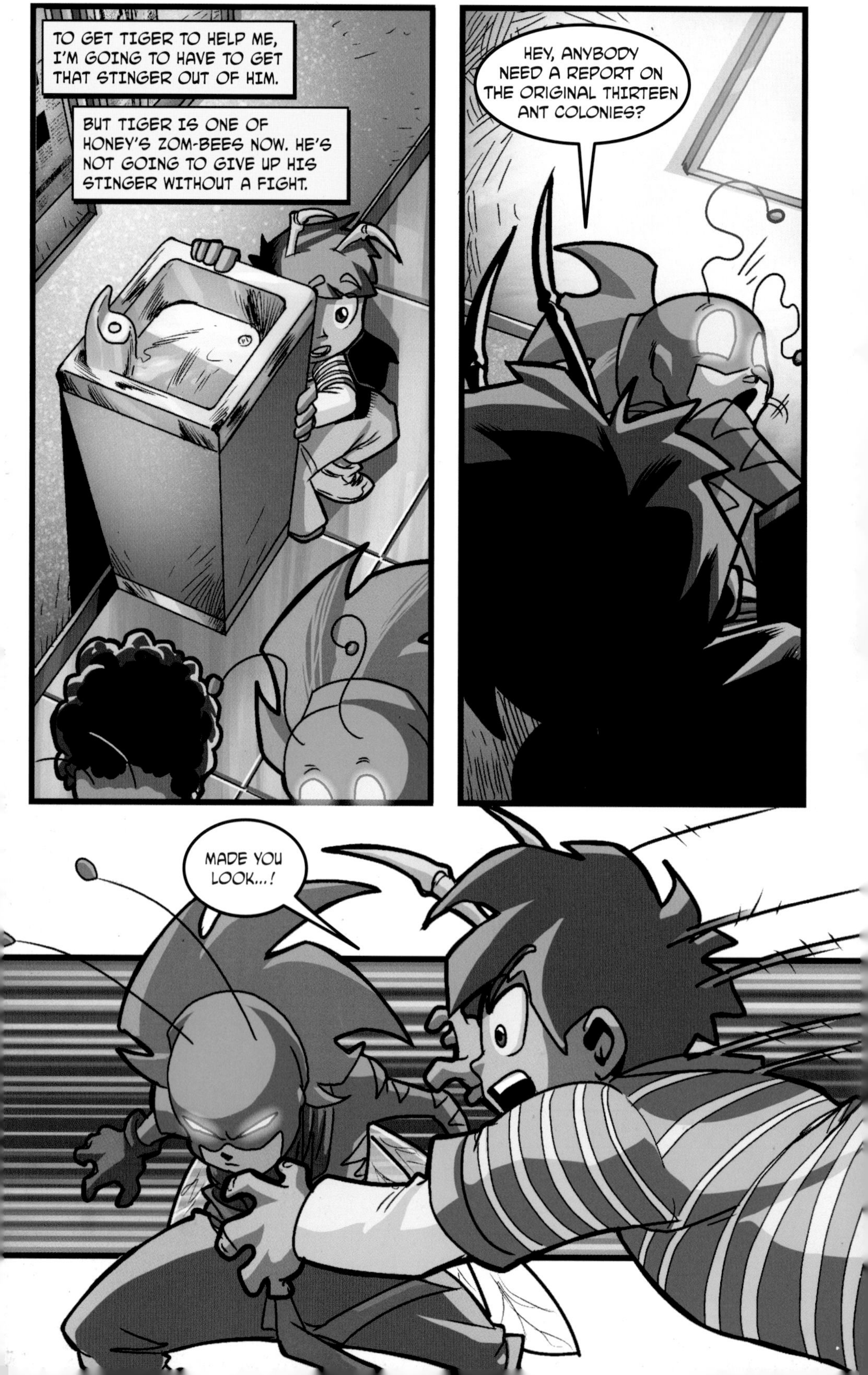
TO GET TIGER TO HELP ME, I'M GOING TO HAVE TO GET THAT STINGER OUT OF HIM.
BUT TIGER IS ONE OF HONEY'S ZOM-BEES NOW. HE'S NOT GOING TO GIVE UP HIS STINGER WITHOUT A FIGHT.
HEY, ANYBODY NEED A REPORT ON THE ORIGINAL THIRTEEN ANT COLONIES?
MADE YOU LOOK...!

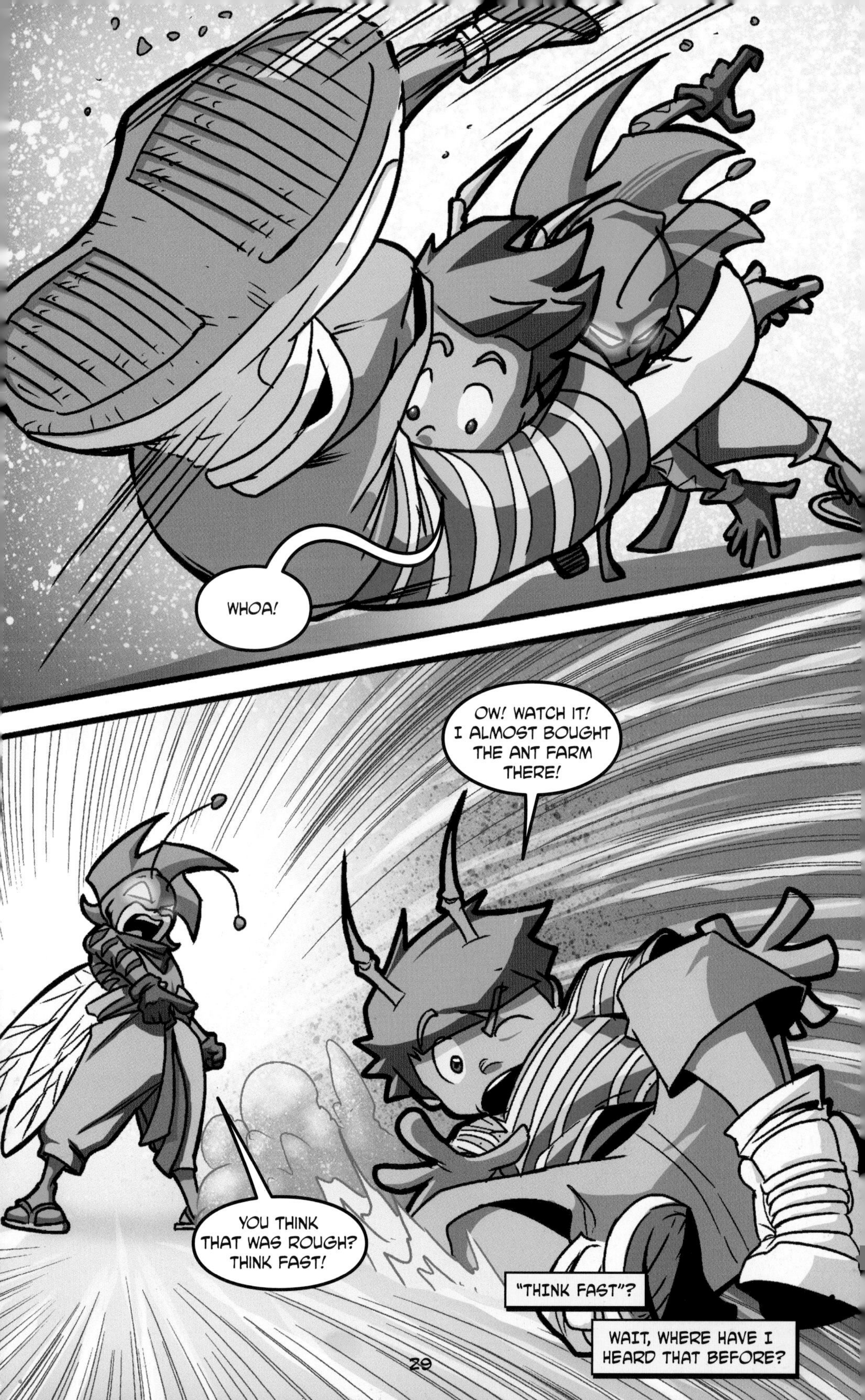
WHOA!
OW! WATCH IT! I ALMOST BOUGHT THE ANT FARM THERE!
YOU THINK THAT WAS ROUGH? THINK FAST!
"THINK FAST"?
WAIT, WHERE HAVE I HEARD THAT BEFORE?

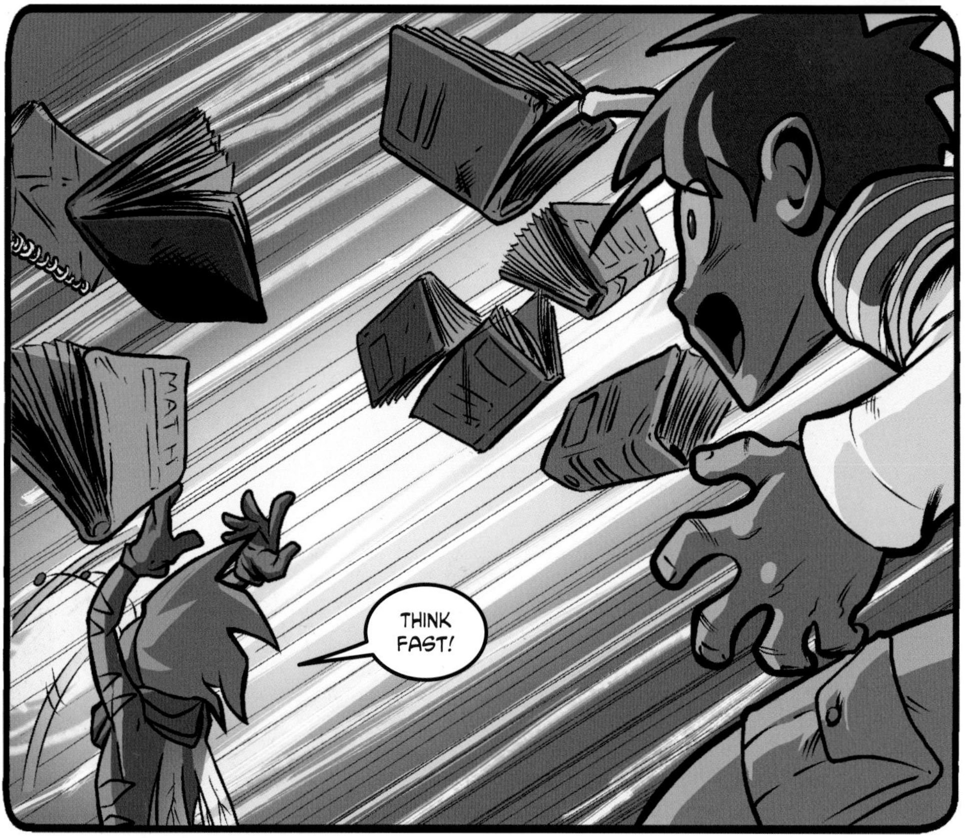
MATH
THINK FAST!

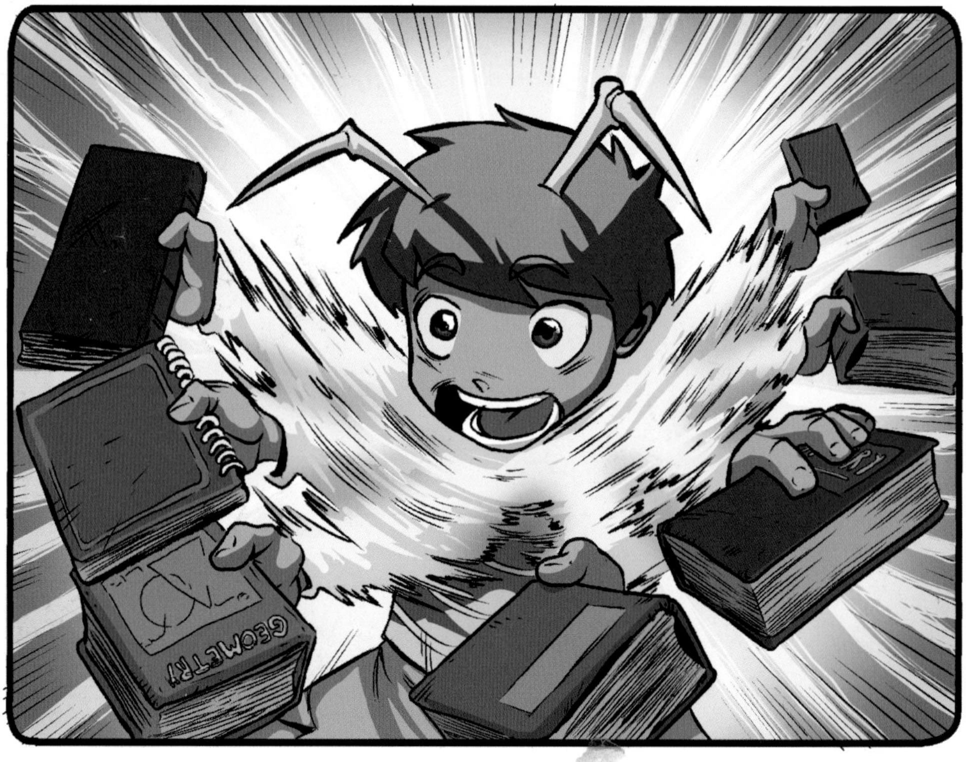
GEOMETRY

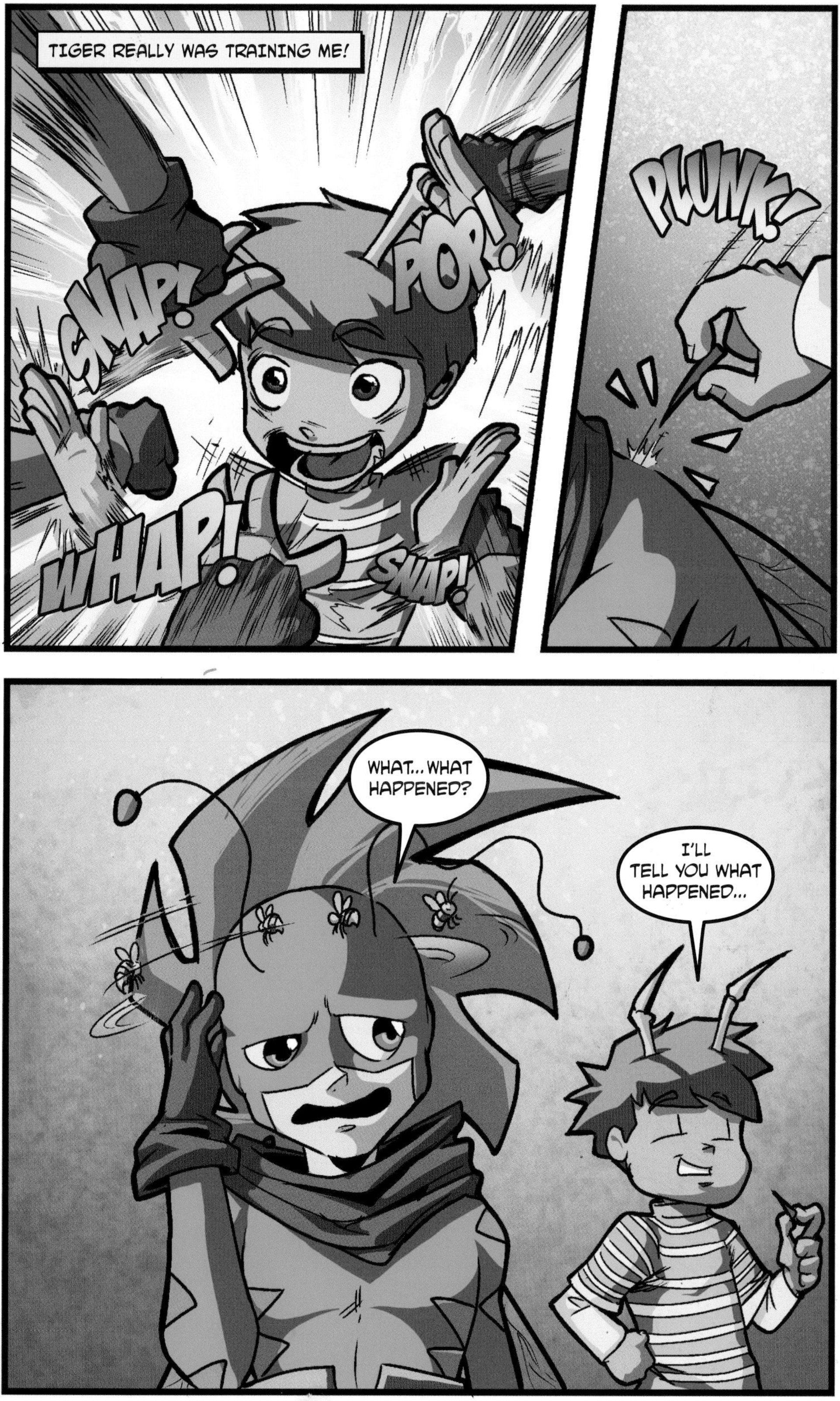
TIGER REALLY WAS TRAINING ME!
SNAP!
POP!
WHAP!
SNAP!
PLUNK!
WHAT...WHAT HAPPENED?
I'LL TELL YOU WHAT HAPPENED...

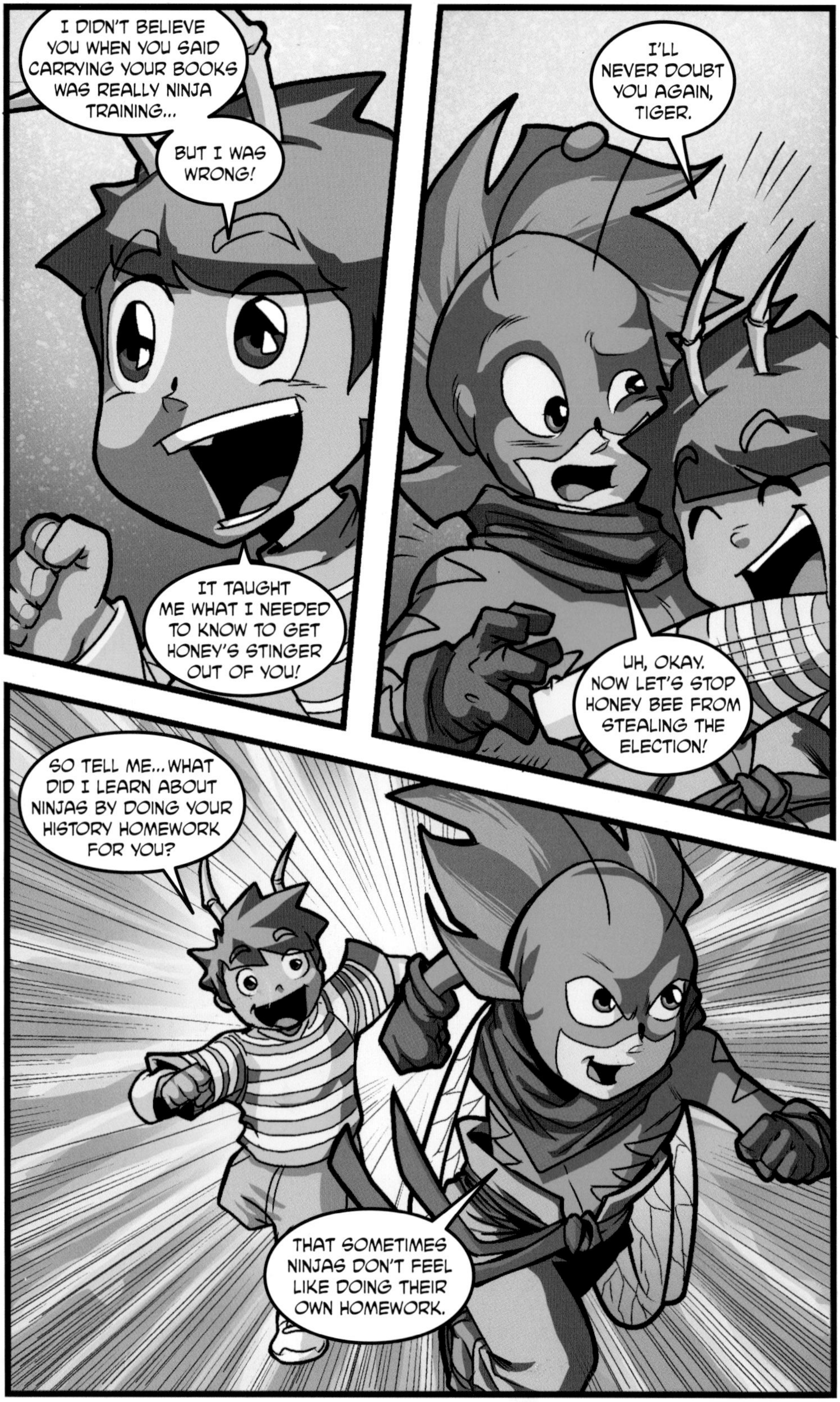
I DIDN'T BELIEVE YOU WHEN YOU SAID CARRYING YOUR BOOKS WAS REALLY NINJA TRAINING...
BUT I WAS WRONG!
IT TAUGHT ME WHAT I NEEDED TO KNOW TO GET HONEY'S STINGER OUT OF YOU!
I'LL NEVER DOUBT YOU AGAIN, TIGER.
UH, OKAY. NOW LET'S STOP HONEY BEE FROM STEALING THE ELECTION!
SO TELL ME... WHAT DID I LEARN ABOUT NINJAS BY DOING YOUR HISTORY HOMEWORK FOR YOU?
THAT SOMETIMES NINJAS DON'T FEEL LIKE DOING THEIR OWN HOMEWORK.

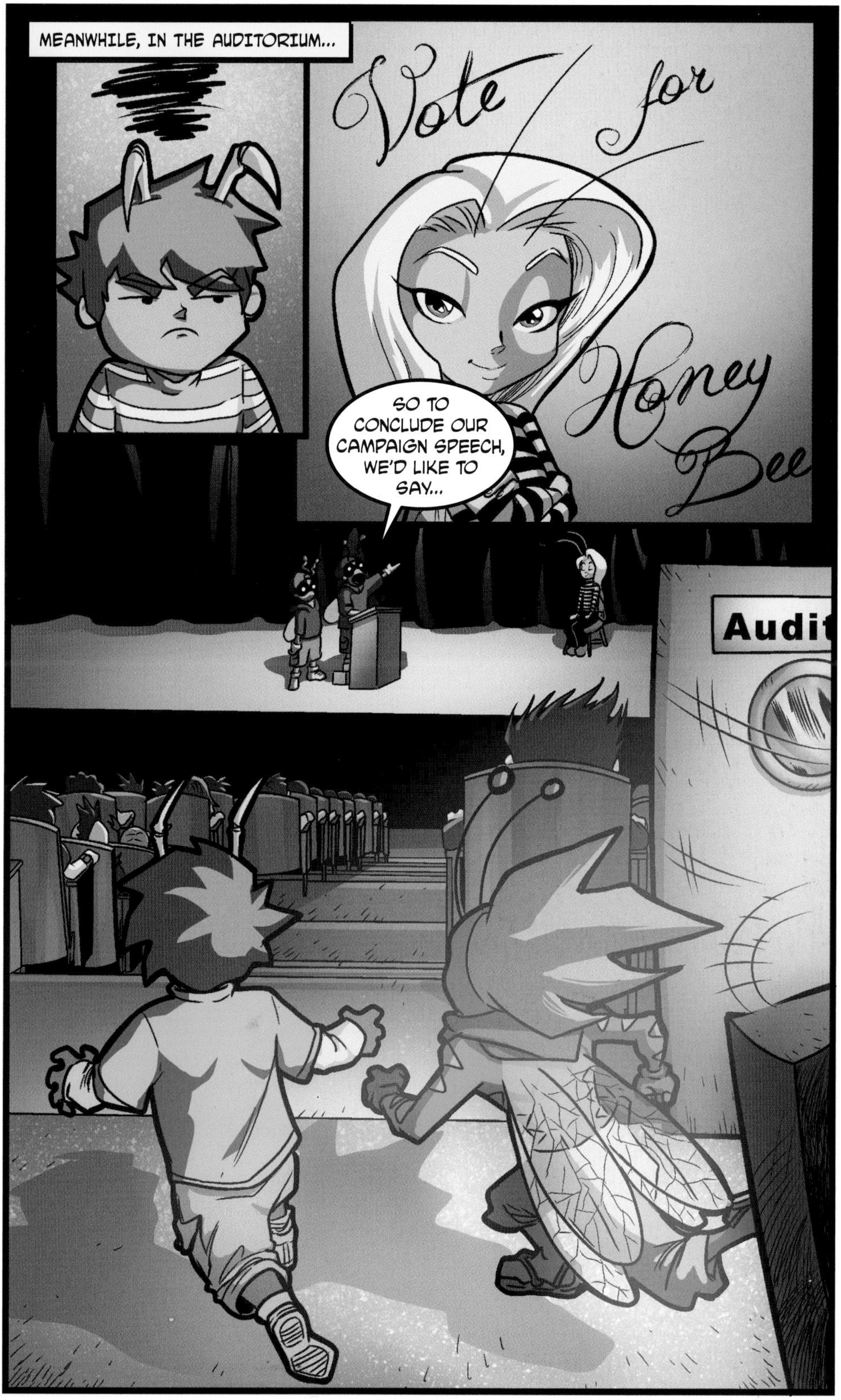
MEANWHILE, IN THE AUDITORIUM...
Vote for Honey Bee
SO TO CONCLUDE OUR CAMPAIGN SPEECH, WE'D LIKE TO SAY...
Audit

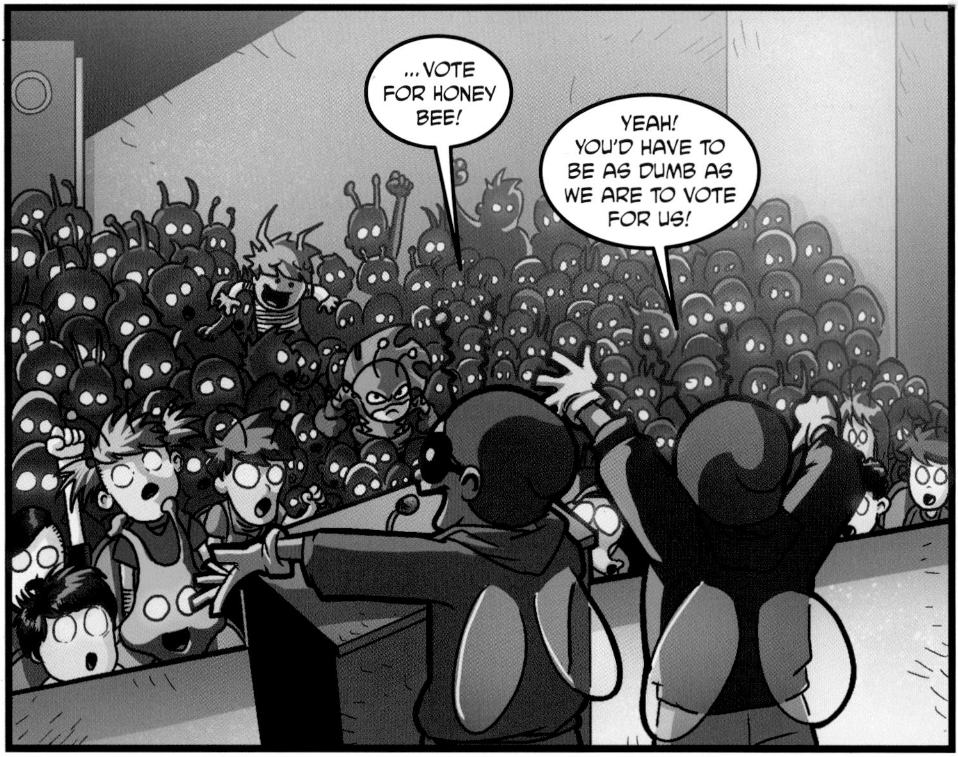
...VOTE FOR HONEY BEE!
YEAH! YOU'D HAVE TO BE AS DUMB AS WE ARE TO VOTE FOR US!

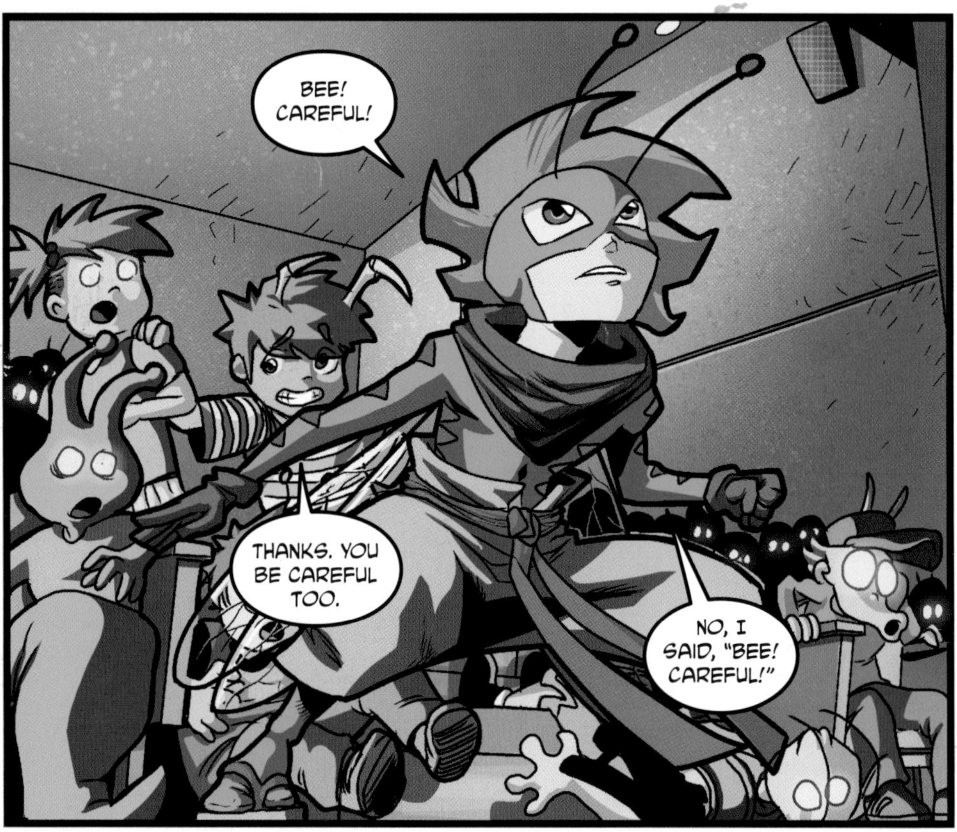
BEE! CAREFUL!
THANKS. YOU BE CAREFUL TOO.
NO, I SAID, "BEE! CAREFUL!"

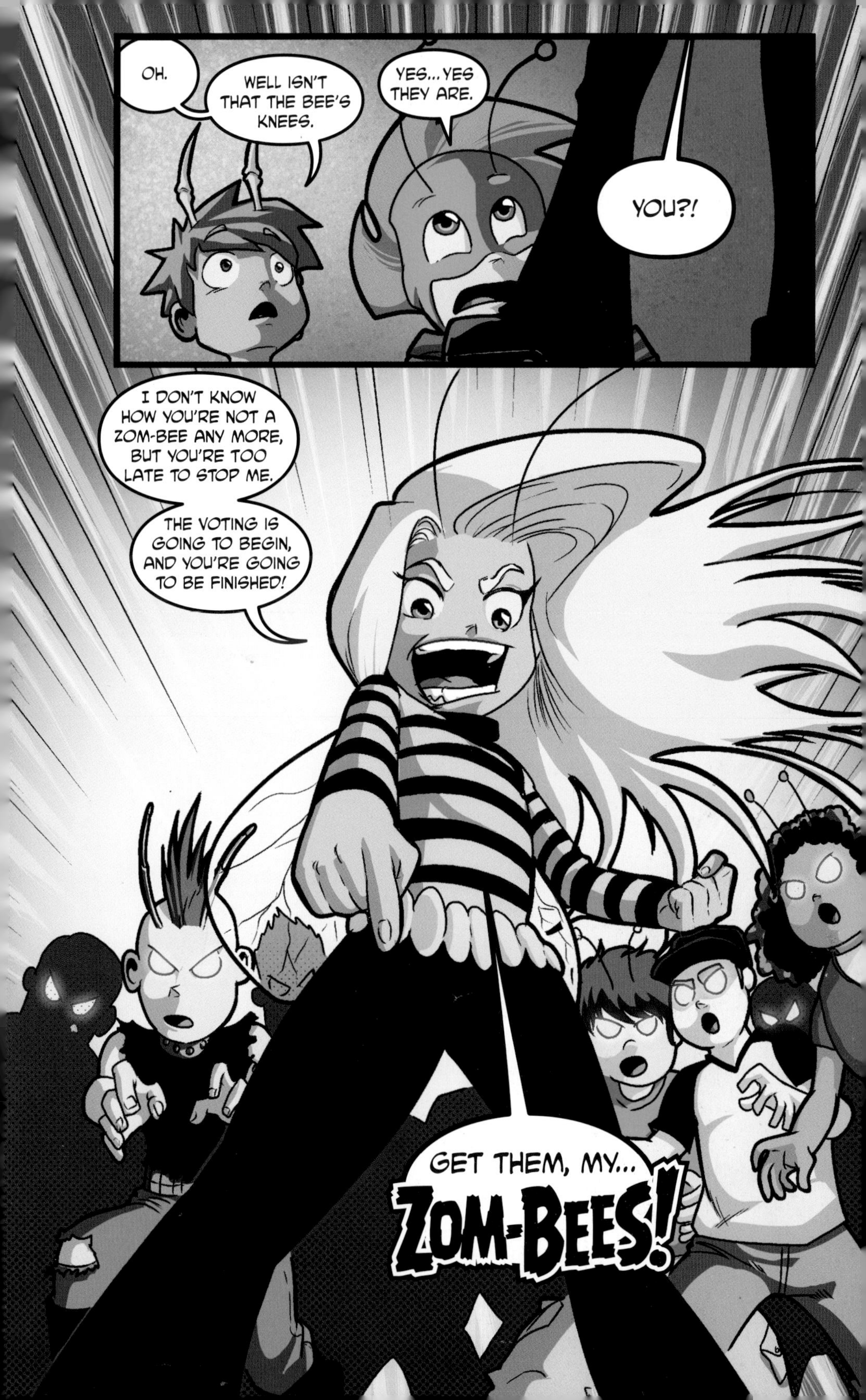
OH.
WELL ISN'T THAT THE BEE'S KNEES.
YES... YES THEY ARE.
YOU?!
I DON'T KNOW HOW YOU'RE NOT A ZOM-BEE ANY MORE, BUT YOU'RE TOO LATE TO STOP ME.
THE VOTING IS GOING TO BEGIN, AND YOU'RE GOING TO BE FINISHED!
GET THEM, MY...
ZOM-BEES!

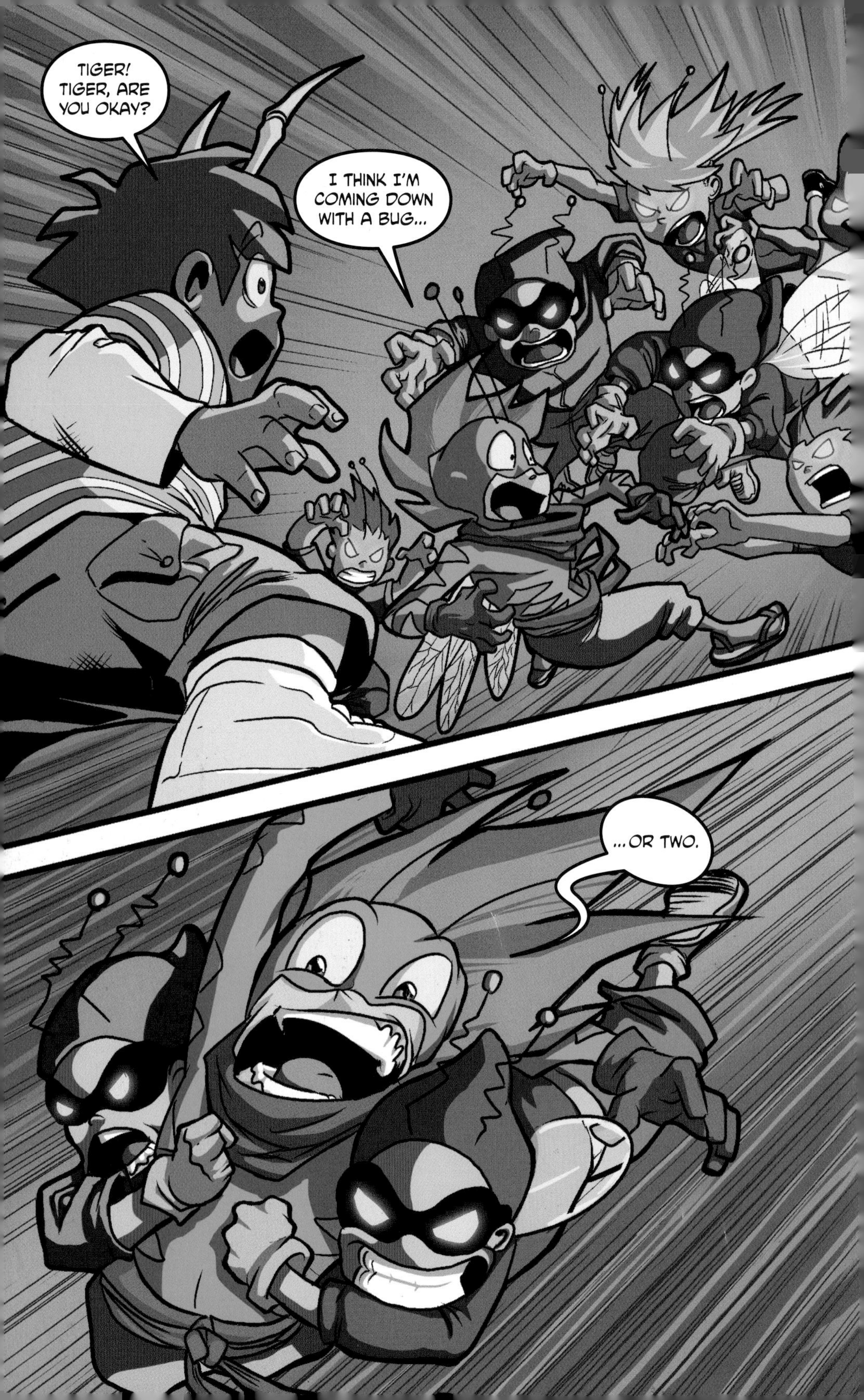
TIGER! TIGER, ARE YOU OKAY?
I THINK I'M COMING DOWN WITH A BUG...
...OR TWO.

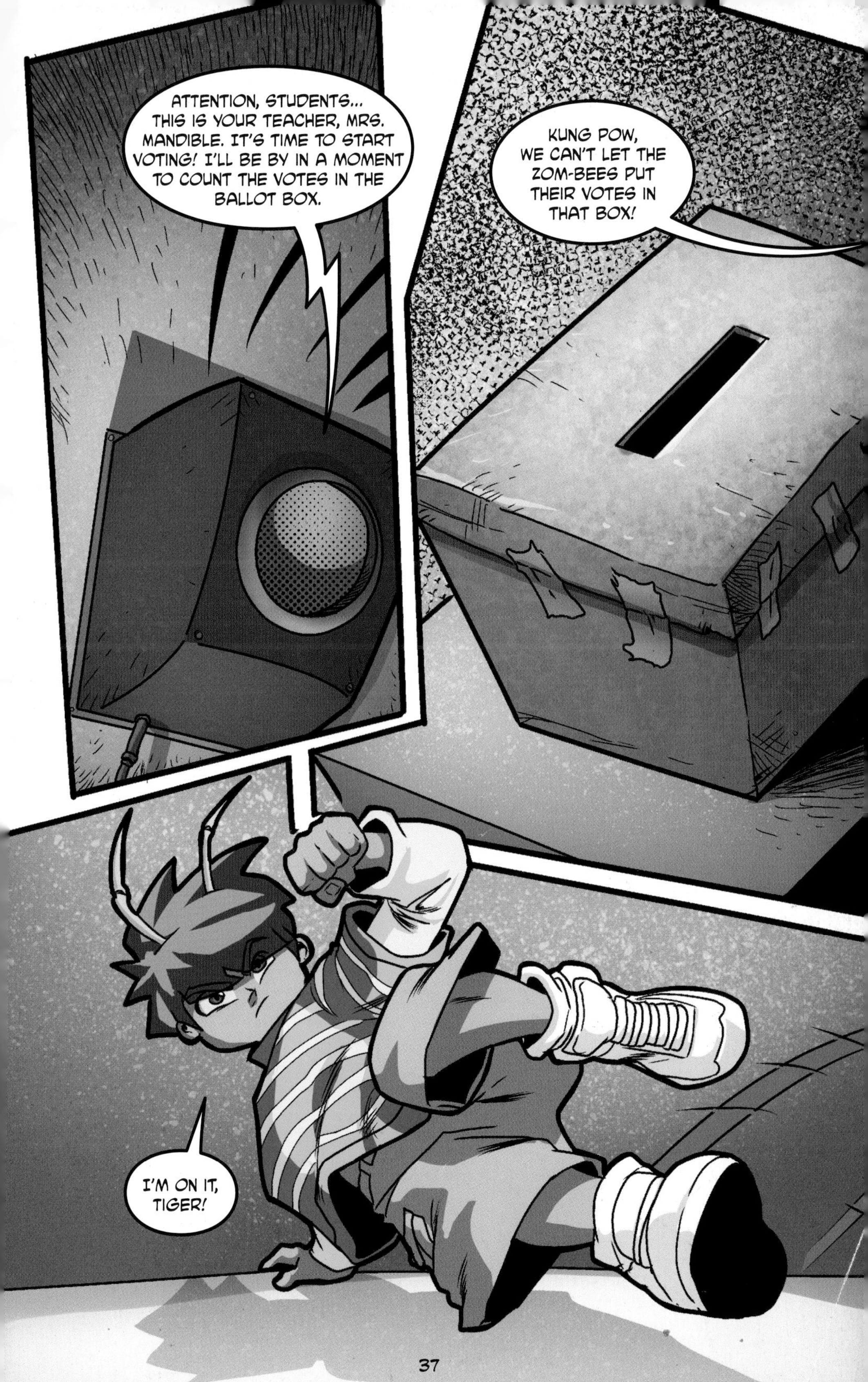
ATTENTION, STUDENTS... THIS IS YOUR TEACHER, MRS. MANDIBLE. IT'S TIME TO START VOTING! I'LL BE BY IN A MOMENT TO COUNT THE VOTES IN THE BALLOT BOX.
KUNG POW, WE CAN'T LET THE ZOM-BEES PUT THEIR VOTES IN THAT BOX!
I'M ON IT, TIGER!

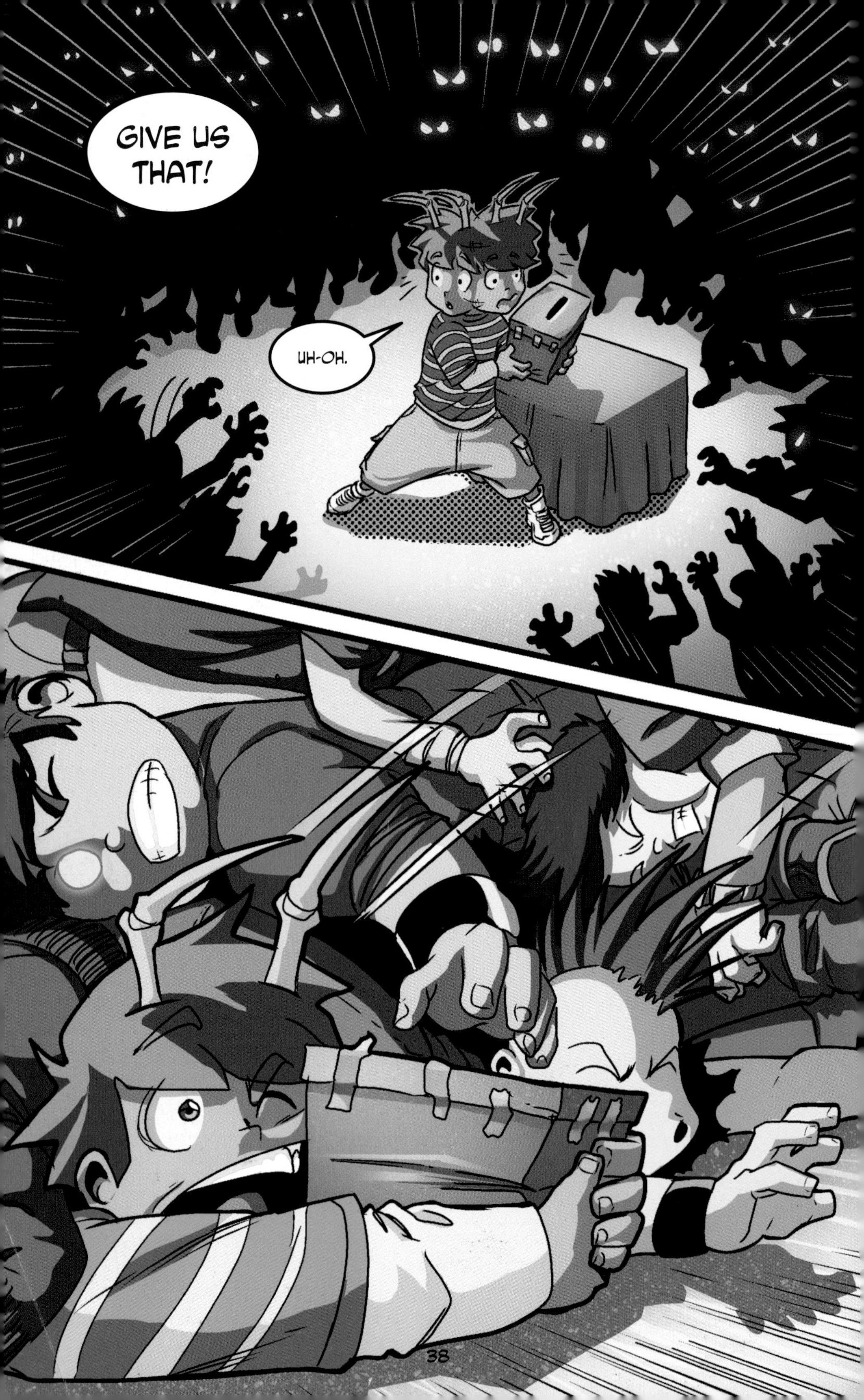
GIVE US THAT!
UH-OH.

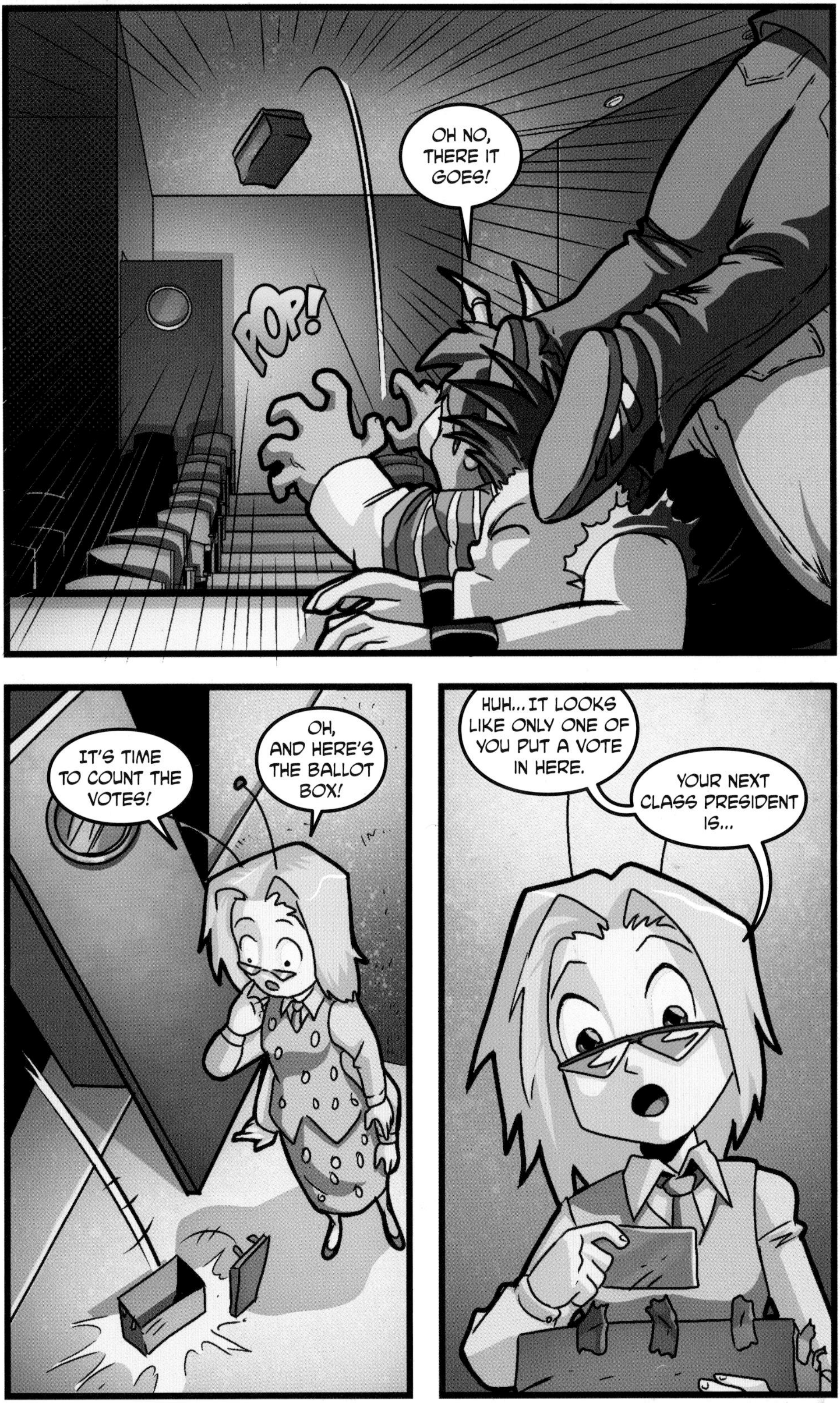
OH NO, THERE IT GOES!
POP!
IT'S TIME TO COUNT THE VOTES!
OH, AND HERE'S THE BALLOT BOX!
HUH... IT LOOKS LIKE ONLY ONE OF YOU PUT A VOTE IN HERE.
YOUR NEXT CLASS PRESIDENT IS...

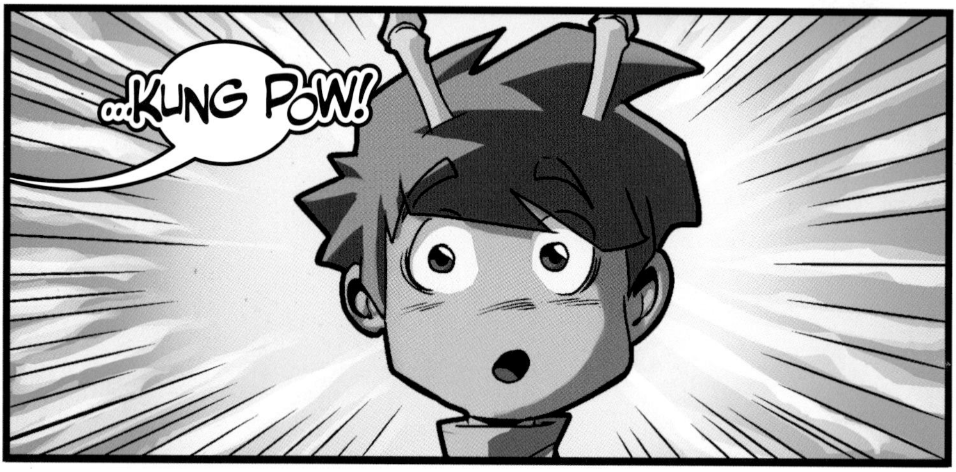
...KUNG POW!

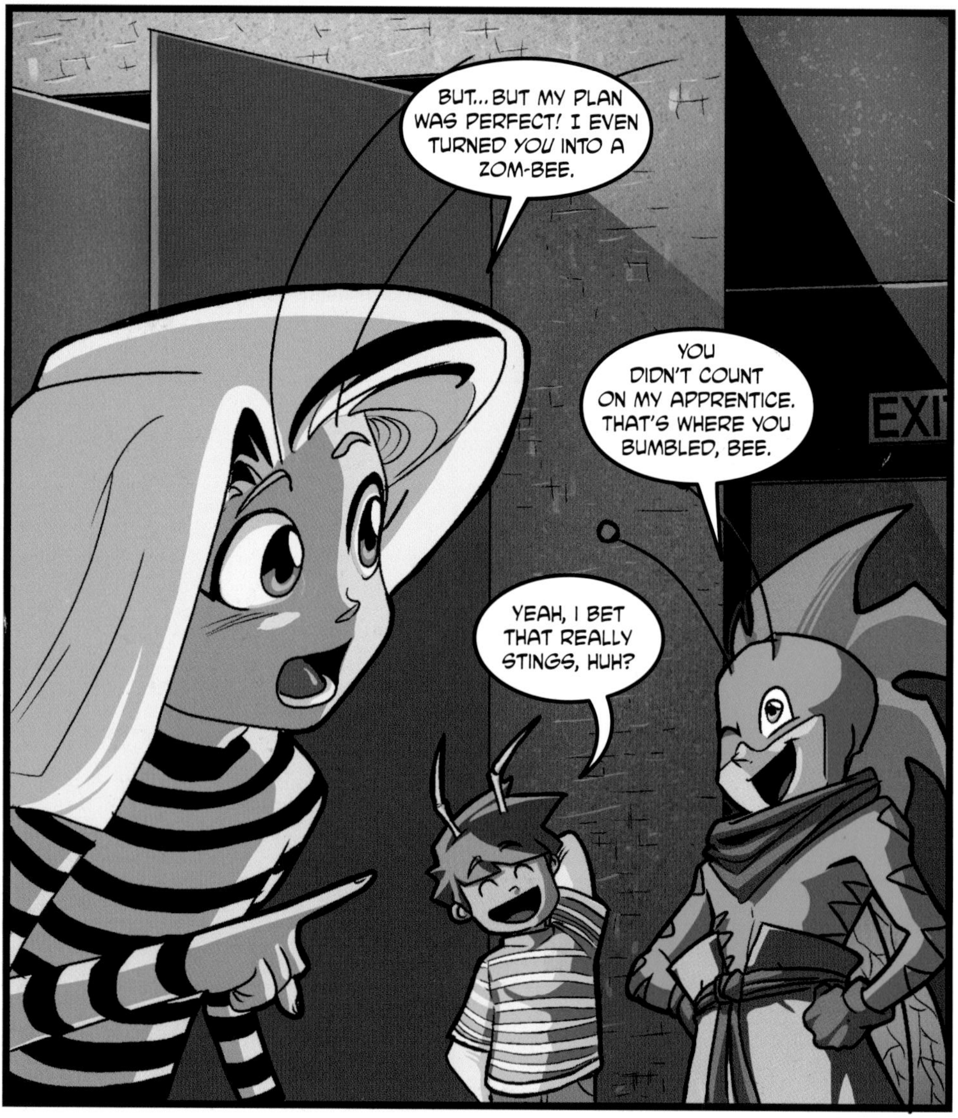
BUT... BUT MY PLAN WAS PERFECT! I EVEN TURNED *YOU* INTO A ZOM-BEE.
YOU DIDN'T COUNT ON MY APPRENTICE. THAT'S WHERE YOU BUMBLED, BEE.
YEAH, I BET THAT REALLY STINGS, HUH?
EXIT

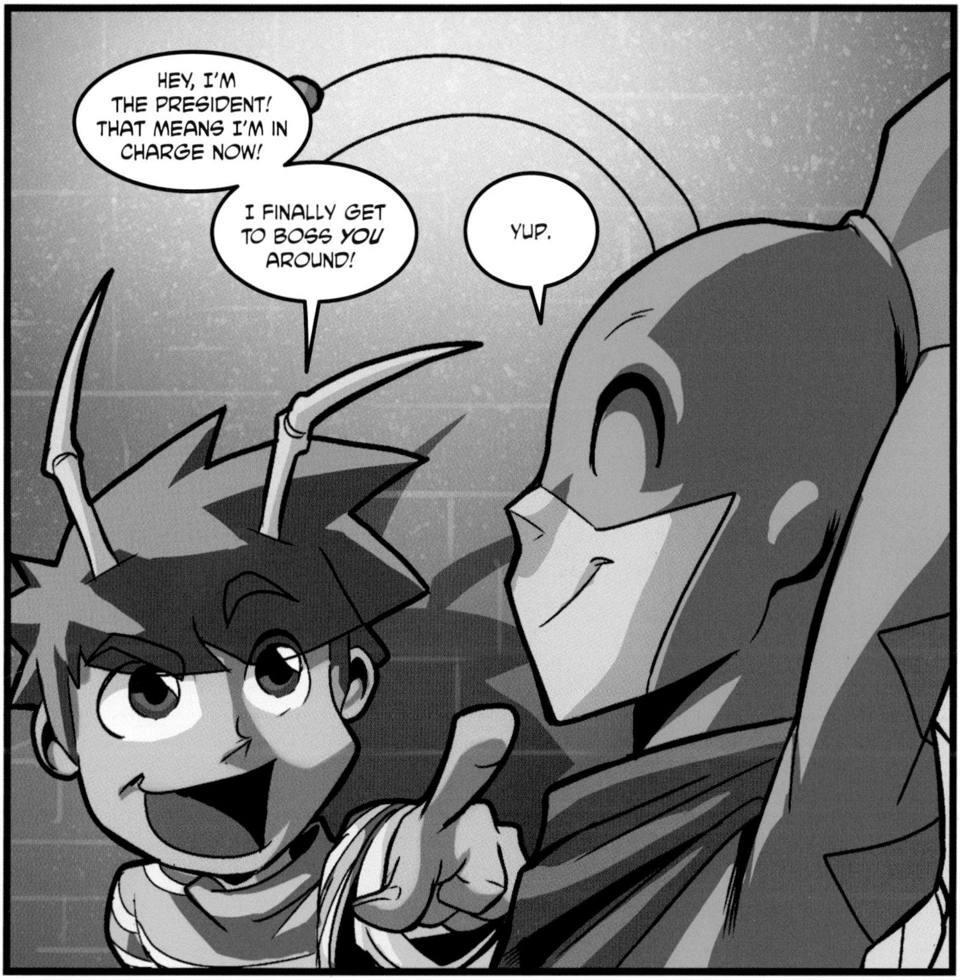
HEY, I'M THE PRESIDENT! THAT MEANS I'M IN CHARGE NOW!
I FINALLY GET TO BOSS *YOU* AROUND!
YUP.

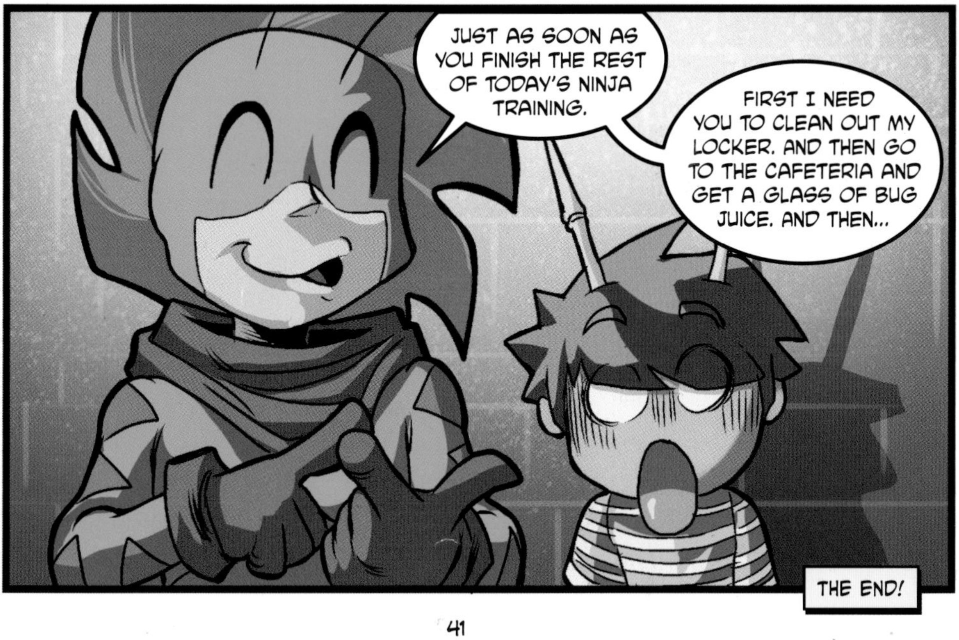
JUST AS SOON AS YOU FINISH THE REST OF TODAY'S NINJA TRAINING.
FIRST I NEED YOU TO CLEAN OUT MY LOCKER. AND THEN GO TO THE CAFETERIA AND GET A GLASS OF BUG JUICE. AND THEN...
THE END!

CREATORS

SCOTT SONNEBORN

Scott Sonneborn has written dozens of books, one circus (for Ringling Bros. Barnum & Bailey), and a bunch of TV shows. He's been nominated for one Emmy and spent three very cool years working at DC Comics. He lives in Los Angeles with his wife and their two sons.

ANDRES ESPARZA

Andres Esparza has been a graphic designer, colorist, and illustrator for many different companies and agencies. Andres now works as a full-time artist for Graphikslava studio in Monterrey, Mexico. In his spare time, Andres loves to play basketball, hang out with family and friends, and listen to good music.

GLOSSARY

apprentice (uh-PREN-tiss)–someone who learns a trade or craft by working with a skilled person

auditorium (aw-di-TOR-ee-uhm)–a building or large room where people gather for events

ballot (BAL-uht)–a secret way of voting, such as on a machine or a slip of paper

bumbled (BUHM-buhld)–mishandled or fouled up

campaign (kam-PAYN)–a series of actions organized over a period of time in order to win an election

candidate (KAN-duh-date)–someone who is applying for a job or running in an election

doubt (DOUT)–to be uncertain about something

hives (HIVES)–a rash that appears on the skin; also a natural structure in which bees build a honeycomb

VISUAL QUESTIONS

1. Comic book illustrators draw motion lines (also known as action lines) to show movement of a character or an object. Find other panels in this book with motion lines. Do you think they make the illustrations more exciting? Explain.

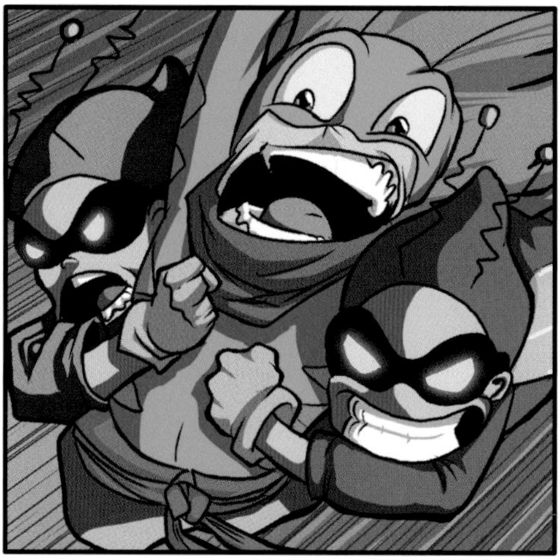

2. The way a character's eyes and mouth look, also known as their facial expression, can tell a lot about the emotions he or she is feeling. How do you think Kung Pow felt in the panel at right from page 40?

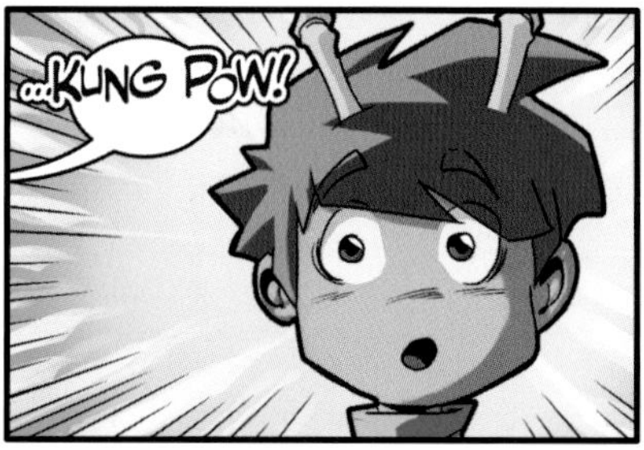
...KUNG POW!

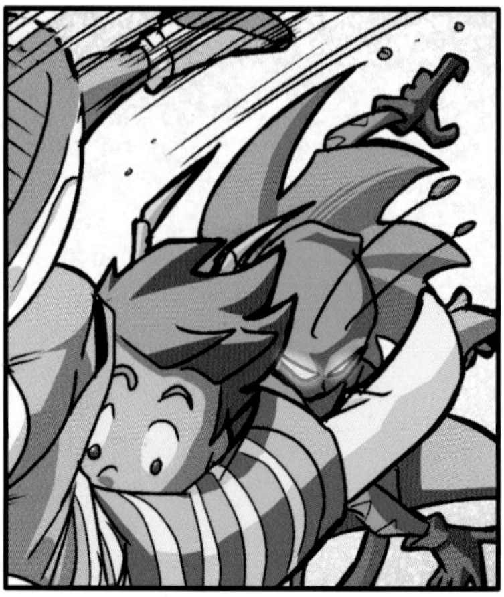

3. Tiger Moth is an expert martial artist. Find at least two panels in this book where the Insect Ninja uses this skill. Do you believe he could've solved those problems differently? Explain your answer.

4. Tiger Moth made Kung Pow carry his books and do his homework. These tasks taught Kung Pow useful ninja skills. Do you think Tiger knew all along that he was teaching Kung Pow this lesson? Explain your answer using examples from the story.

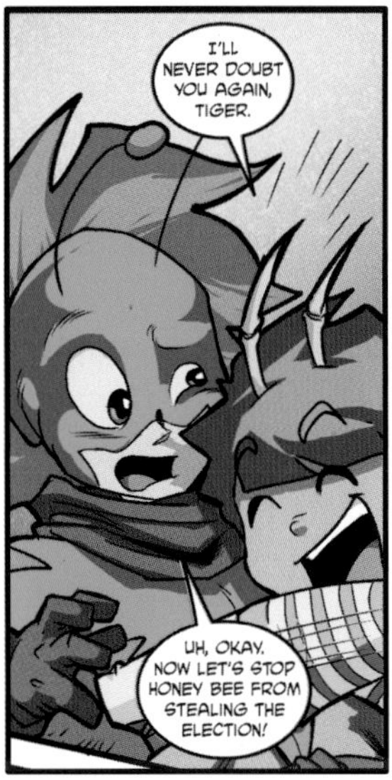
I'LL NEVER DOUBT YOU AGAIN, TIGER.
UH, OKAY. NOW LET'S STOP HONEY BEE FROM STEALING THE ELECTION!

5. In comic books, sound effects (also known as SFX) are used to show sounds, such as the firing of a gun or other weapon. Make a list of all the sound effects in this book, and then write a definition for each term. Soon, you'll have your own SFX dictionary!

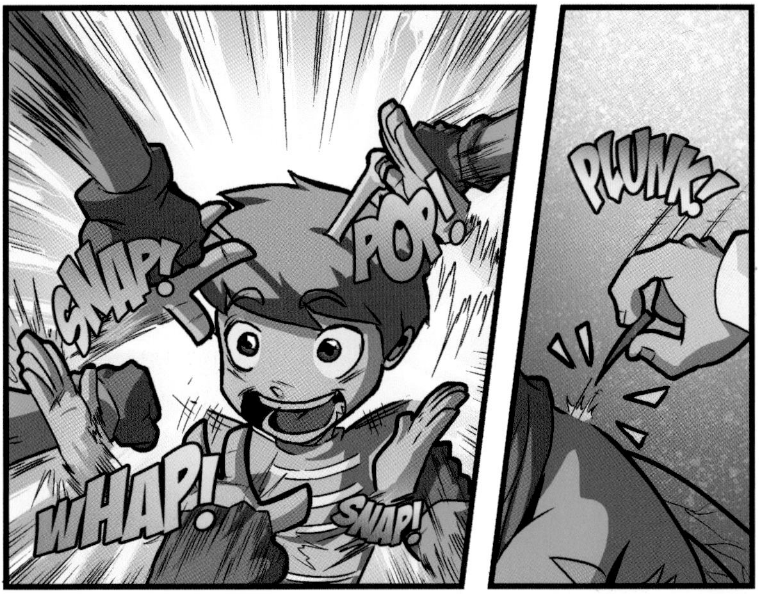
SNAP!
POP!
WHAP!
SNAP!
PLUNK!

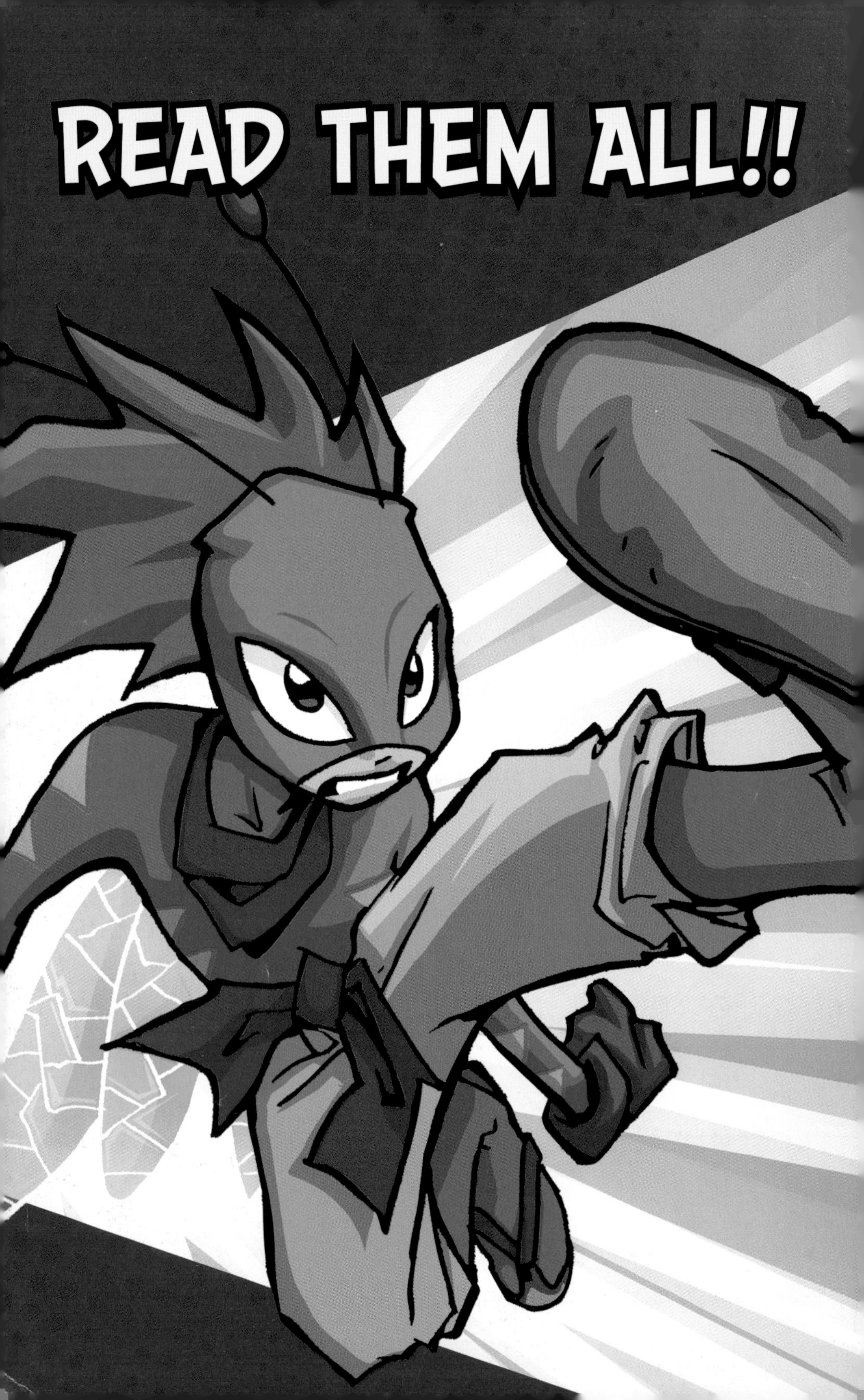
READ THEM ALL!!

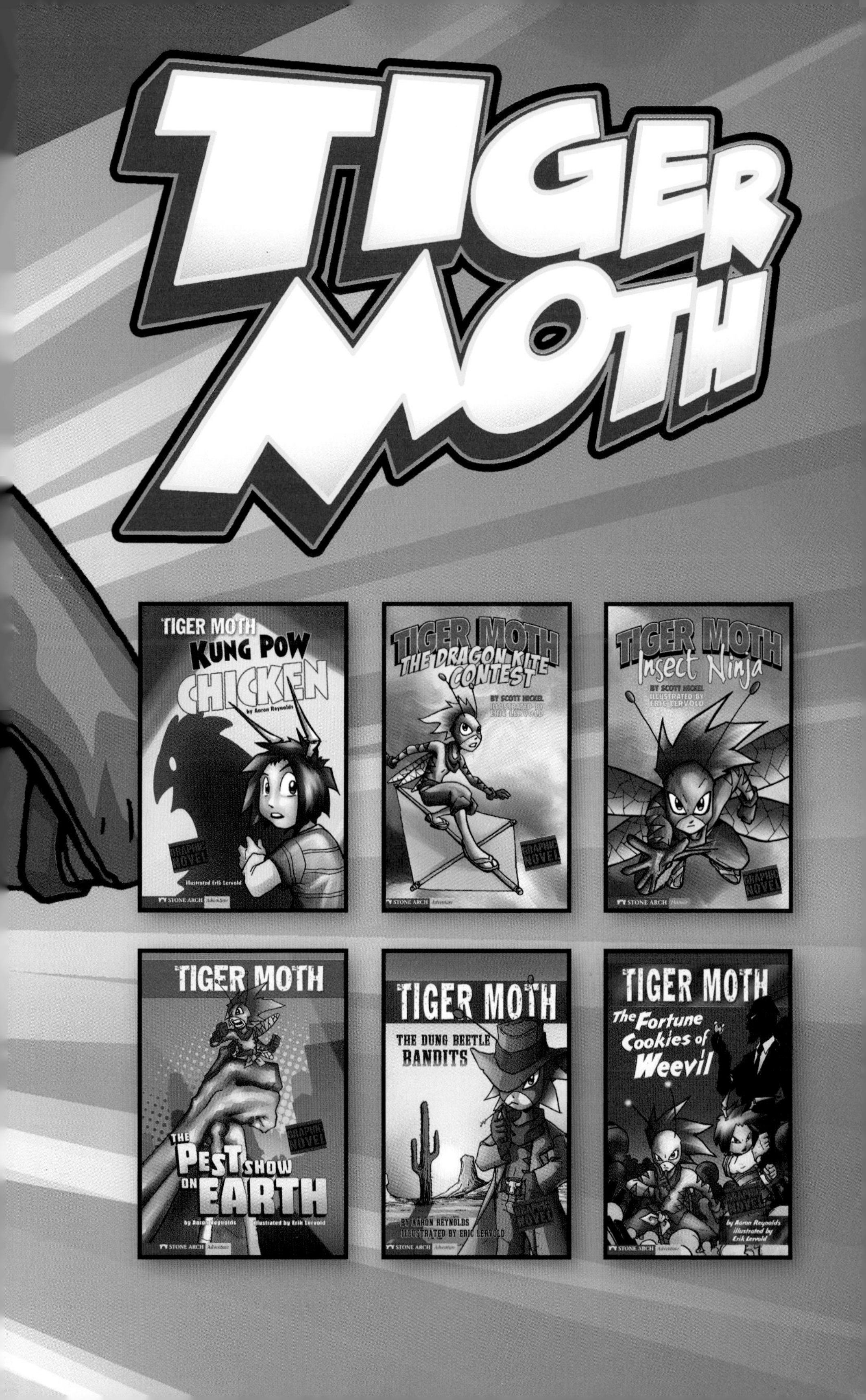
TIGER MOTH
TIGER MOTH
KUNG POW CHICKEN
by Aaron Reynolds
GRAPHIC NOVEL
illustrated Erik Lervold
STONE ARCH Adventure
TIGER MOTH
THE DRAGON KITE CONTEST
BY SCOTT NICKEL
ILLUSTRATED BY ERIC LERVOLD
GRAPHIC NOVEL
STONE ARCH Adventure
TIGER MOTH
Insect Ninja
BY SCOTT NICKEL
ILLUSTRATED BY ERIC LERVOLD
GRAPHIC NOVEL
STONE ARCH Humor
TIGER MOTH
GRAPHIC NOVEL
THE PEST SHOW ON EARTH
by Aaron Reynolds
illustrated by Erik Lervold
STONE ARCH Adventure
TIGER MOTH
THE DUNG BEETLE BANDITS
BY AARON REYNOLDS
ILLUSTRATED BY ERIC LERVOLD
STONE ARCH Adventure
TIGER MOTH
The Fortune Cookies of Weevil
by Aaron Reynolds
illustrated by Erik Lervold
STONE ARCH Adventure

THE FUN DOESN'T STOP HERE!

DISCOVER MORE AT...

WWW.CAPSTONEKIDS.COM

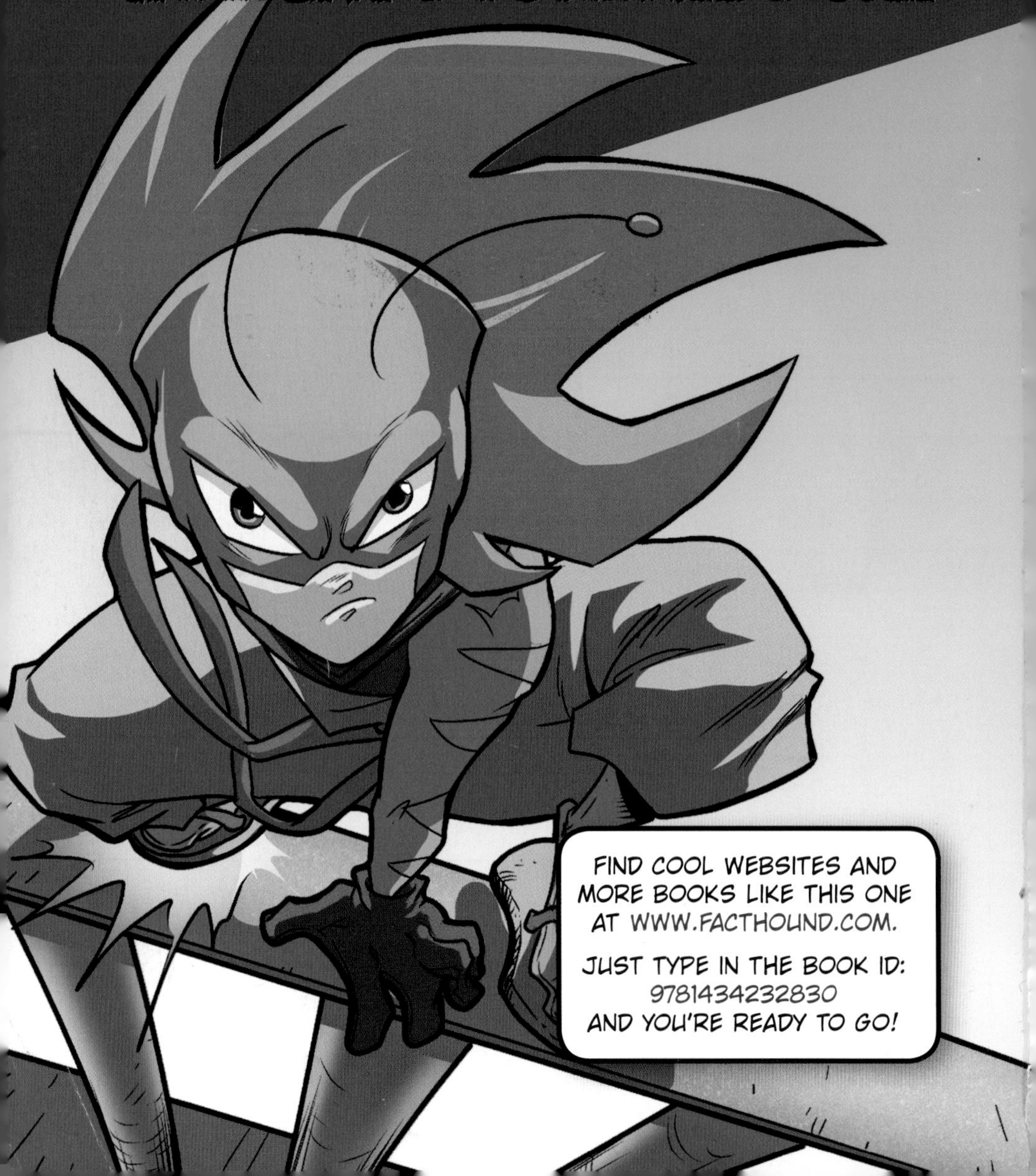

FIND COOL WEBSITES AND MORE BOOKS LIKE THIS ONE AT WWW.FACTHOUND.COM.

JUST TYPE IN THE BOOK ID: 9781434232830 AND YOU'RE READY TO GO!